THE SECRET BUNKER 3

REGENERATION

PAUL TEAGUE

INTRODUCTION

This trilogy of books was inspired by a family visit to Scotland's Secret Bunker which is located at Troywood in Fife, Scotland, UK, however, it is entirely fictional.

If you get the chance, please visit to the real 'Secret Bunker' it's an amazing place!

This book has been fully revised and updated to mark the 25th anniversary of Scotland's Secret Bunker being open to the public.

You can find out more about the bunker at https://www.secretbunker.co.uk/

ALSO BY PAUL TEAGUE

Sci-Fi Starter Book - Phase 6

The Grid Trilogy

Book 1 - Fall of Justice

Book 2 - Quest for Vengeance

Book 3 - Catharsis

With Jon Evans

Book 1 - Incursion

Book 2 - Armada

Book 3 - Devastation

PROLOGUE

Nemesis

The severed hand flew across the wet, dark mine shaft leaving a streak of blood on the rocky floor where it came to rest at the feet of the protesting miners. As the sword had struck his wrist, he'd stifled a scream, instantly burying the horror and pain of what was happening for fear of losing his head as well.

This was the Helyion way. They were used to terror. But the miners had also been present at a defining moment in their planet's history.

They were angry about the long hours they were being forced to work deep underground. The planet was dying, mineral resources severely depleted and their people at risk of extinction. Of course they realized it was paramount to increase output and endure extended shift times to create the materials that would help to progress off-world exploration. Humanity's one hope lay among the planets beyond Helyios 4, the entire population understood that. But a young commander, hungry for success, had taken things too far. He'd seen opportunity in the present crisis, a chance to rise above his humble beginnings living in poverty with a father too drunk to work. His perfectly honed sense of timing and strategy had told him that in this potential disaster lay the chance to make a name for himself. The Helyion Congress required raw materials and they didn't want to wait. They made the right noises about looking after the interests of their people and wanting the best outcomes for them, but they also knew the stark truth. This planet would soon be dead. The end might come within this or the next generation. So, although it was crucial to maintain consensus and discipline, there was also work to be done.

When the young Helyion had taken charge of the most important mine in the sector – after a mysterious and unfortunate accident resulting in the sudden death of his predecessor – productivity had soared. He'd immediately come to the attention of the most senior members of the Helyion Congress. Here was a commander, finally, who understood the need for results. Fast results, at any cost.

When his team of miners had protested about working practices and safety issues, he'd had two choices. Either he could listen to their concerns, show them he'd taken them into account and would make the changes that they were requesting. Or, with a sudden outburst of fury and violence, he could forever quash any further challenges to his authority, in an instant showing the decisiveness and leadership qualities that would cause this particular Helyion to soar rapidly through the ranks of commanders.

So, the young Zadra Nurmeen sliced off the hand of the protesting miner, thus securing total dominance over the workers under his cruel leadership. The sudden, ruthless swipe of his weapon, drawn rapidly from a concealed sheath slung across his back, secured his meteoric rise through the Helyion ranks.

He would eventually become a feared and influential leader, yet always he would carry that weapon hidden on his person. It was the same sword that many years later would be violently swung at the neck of a young human called Dan Tracy in the final moments which would define the fate of another planet called Earth.

Deal

The deal was done – it was sealed by a handshake. They had been disowned by the leaders who had once celebrated their wisdom. Both harboured grudges against the very people who had previously been their friends and colleagues. Deep inside, they incubated a contempt of humanity, an unstoppable urge to destroy and dominate.

There were many buyers interested in the planet known as Earth. As it was, inhabited by a vast array of different species, it was untouchable under interplanetary laws. But if the terraforming went wrong, if the planet were to die?

Well, that would be another story.

The Queen

The troopers worked as one, controlled by the Queen. She was all powerful, they never thought to question her commands. They would receive their instructions via the black devices buried within their necks.

They had been culled from humanity, the finest physical specimens enhanced by incredible technology. All answerable to their Queen, who was part of this unholy trinity. But nobody knew who she was. She was able to control this dangerous army with complete anonymity. And so it would remain until the final battle.

Launch

He took a deep breath as he carefully keyed in the coordinates sketched out on his console. He had been here before, where life and death were precariously balanced on a knife-edge and brave decisions and terrible risks had to be taken to preserve lives.

But who knew how things would play out if these missiles reached their targets?

He confirmed the coordinates and it was done.

Deep beneath the Black Sea, fifty submarine drones were armed in an instant. Each one carried a massive nuclear payload. Within the hour they would reach their final destination.

Birth

The twins were beautiful. They looked exactly like the doctor said they would. The human genes were dominant – they would blend in seamlessly on this planet. They would remain undetected, able to live a normal life. Each was perfectly formed, a boy and a girl.

But she would be compelled to abandon her children on Earth and trust the humans to show them the kindness they had offered to herself and her husband. She had to return to her own planet to face trial by the elders. She had committed the ultimate crime. She had revealed to the humans that there was life elsewhere among the stars.

CHAPTER ONE

Three Hours

Everybody looked shocked as Xiang delivered the devastating news about our imminent genetic destruction. We had three hours to live ... three hours to fix this thing or die at the hands of a deadly nanovirus.

We were all desperately concerned about James, and for a short time we were at a loss as to which problem to concentrate on. Nat was the first to break the silence. When we were parted by the accident I'm certain neither of us knew language like she was using now. In fact, I'm sure she used a few words that I still don't know as she described her hatred of Doctor Pierce.

Not for the first time that day I felt calm and levelheaded in the face of extreme stress. I broke into Nat's tirade.

'So we need to move fast. How will this nano thing work when it kicks in, Xiang?'

Nat stopped her ranting. She was obviously angry and

frustrated, but like me she was also focused on how we could stop this genetic sabotage.

'I feel fine at the moment,' she said, embarrassed by her outburst as she realized everybody had been watching her tantrum.

'How come I seem to be more advanced than Dan in the viral process, Xiang?' she added, mastering her temper at last.

That was a good question and I felt exactly the same way. I hadn't felt so healthy in years.

Xiang pressed a few keys on her E-Pad and a graphic appeared on the main screen in the briefing room. After the relief of Dad's good news about the drones, the atmosphere was tense once again. There were two graphical images of bodies – me and Nat, I guessed. Xiang talked us through the science bit. The technical words sounded like 'blah, blah, blah' to me, but I got the gist. Essentially our bodies were like two boilers. When they both reached full pressure, they'd explode. Only there was no gas involved here, it was a genetic process. And the two boilers in question were me and Nat. We'd continue to function until we both hit that critical mass. One boiler wouldn't explode before the other. When the process was complete in both of us ... boom! Except there wouldn't be an explosion. Nat and I would just die. The process would effectively mean that we'd cancel each other out, we would devour each other – genetically speaking. What a reunion!

Xiang sent the data to our comms tabs so we could monitor the process of genetic breakdown and the time we had left. Nat was at 66.5 percent in the process, I was at 35 percent. That wasn't comforting me. She had monitored and simulated the speed of the viral process via nano-trackers inserted into our bloodstreams during the earlier tests. So far she thought we had three hours and two minutes before we both reached the 100 percent stage. That would be the end for both of us. To think that the first time I'd ever get to a 100 percent score would also be the last time it ever happened. Darn! Typical Dan Tracy luck.

The counter showing the time remaining kept fluctuating on my comms tab – at times it was as low as two hours and forty-nine minutes. It was a bit like the gauge on a car dashboard projecting how many miles were left until you ran out of fuel, but constantly varying dependent on your speed.

'What accelerates or slows down the process, Xiang? Any idea?' asked Dad.

'I'm not sure yet,' she replied. She was winging all of this like the rest of us. 'With your permission, Dan and Nat, I want to re-route your vital signs via your comms tabs so I can figure out what makes the process speed up. If we can isolate those factors, we may be able to buy you more time.'

Mum stepped in. She'd been quiet since we lost contact with James, but she was obviously thinking things through, coming to terms with recent events in her own way. Simon was trying to find out what had happened to James. We were still waiting to get a full update after the mast was blown up outside, and the teams in the control room were frantically trying to piece it together from whatever information they could access. Mum began to speak. She was controlled, but angry.

'Now the drones have been stopped, we need to go on the offensive against Quadrant 1. We're just sitting ducks here.' There were nods around the table. 'The primary problem is Kate and those troops of hers. If we go on the offensive and manage to stop them we can solve most of our problems.'

Viktor was the outsider here. He'd only just been introduced to this group of ours, and he'd been biding his time, weighing up the room and picking his moment to speak. He seemed to have been waiting for the words 'go on the offensive'. He stood up to get our attention as he spoke.

'We have access to nuclear devices,' he said gravely. 'If we need to, we can blow them out of the ground, like they tried to do to us.'

The mood in the room changed suddenly. It dawned on all of us that we were talking about some big concepts here. One minute you're on a day trip, the next you're deciding where to fire the nukes. I hadn't even had time to buy anything from the gift shop.

Magnus spoke. He didn't like this at all. The tension in the room was increasing – this ramshackle government of ours couldn't agree on the way ahead. It didn't matter anyway, because as the conversations started to heat up and everybody tried to have their say at once there was a deep, menacing rumble throughout the entire bunker. It was sustained and thunderous, more threatening than the drones that had been firing at us before.

The room was silenced. We looked at each other. The fear on everybody's faces told the whole story. Nat and I may not have to worry about the next three hours, it was what was happening right now that might kill us.

Undetected

Kate was severely disorientated. She'd been conscious through everything that had gone on in the bunker so far. As with Amy and James, the device implanted in her neck worked at a subtle level. It controlled her actions, emotions and words but didn't disable her memories or awareness. It was if she'd suddenly awoken from a dream and was having to realign her sense of reality, working through what was part of the dream and what was real.

All around her were bunker staff who were experiencing the same sensations. Like Kate, they'd had the neuronic devices implanted prior to this mission. When James destroyed the mobile mast above them the sabotaged signals had been terminated and they were all left in a similar state of confusion.

Standing around the control room, like a threatening invading force, were the troopers, armed, deadly, and on a mission to destroy the planet. Kate made her decision in an instant. This was the same decisiveness that had resulted in her standing out to Doctor Pierce all those years ago in the simulation exercise. It's why she was here in this bunker now – because of the kind of person she was.

Kate knew she'd have a very short time between regaining her full consciousness and the troopers – or Doctor Pierce – realizing that the bunker staff were no longer under their control. She couldn't save everybody here, but she could get out herself and maybe give the people in the only unoccupied Quadrant a head start in fighting back. If she could make contact with the other Quadrants, the intelligence she could give them might put right some of the damage she'd unleashed under the control of the neural implant.

She used a distraction strategy. Data was streaming in about the explosion close to the cottage above ground. She shouted orders at the troopers and immediately they moved to start investigating what had happened. Of course, they'd find out that James had just blown up the mobile mast which controlled the bunker staff, but Kate would be gone by then.

Having busied the troopers, she walked up to her deputy and whispered in his ear.

'You're in charge, Alan. Make sure you protect the bunker staff when they realize what's going on.'

He nodded.

'I'm leaving you now, but I'll be back … just make sure that you keep these people alive!'

Trapped

'James!' shouted Simon via his comms tab. 'James, are you okay?'

Simon couldn't be sure if his friend been caught by the blast from the explosion or if the sound of weapon fire meant that the troopers had wounded or even killed him. Stuck near the blast doors, he had to find out what had happened. He couldn't go outside, but he could wait for the troopers to re-enter the bunker, possibly with James apprehended. He needed to take the initiative and find out what was going on.

He still had basic clearance in the bunker. He needed to head to the control room, this is where the data would be flowing in about the explosion – and the fate of James. He made his way along the corridor, bowing his head as he passed cameras and troopers. They were all over the place, swarming like ants. Knowing what he knew about Genesis 2, they had to be a product of the Global Consortium. Simon had never seen anything like this before. This was definitely not his access level.

Making his way down towards the control room, the elevator stopped on Level 2. Simon dipped his head, ready to avoid eye contact. Someone stepped into the elevator. It couldn't have been worse. He was trapped in there with Kate. She was looking directly at him. And she'd recognized him immediately.

CHAPTER TWO

Host

The Queen was not among her soldiers, she was many hundreds of thousands of kilometres away, alone in space, connected to a vast array of computers, alongside hundreds of screens and panels. Electrodes were attached to her entire body and wires ran to and from her skull, directly connecting to different parts of her brain. She did not seem to be awake, yet her eyes were open. She had the appearance of being in the middle of a troubling dream, she was restless and agitated.

Around her the screens showed a constant flow of data – she was in direct communication with her troopers, wired into their consciousness, creating a hub that thought and acted as one.

Although she was a captive here, this prison had once offered her food, water, recreation and comfort. Now it had become a living hell. The abomination that had been inflicted upon her looked like a botched job lashed up by a crazed professor. She could not move – she was completely paralysed by this inhuman and torturous process which was using her body as a host and which would eventually leave her lifeless. Somebody had done this to her, someone who was deeply evil and had no compassion or respect for life. From this lonely place the Queen had been chosen to preside over the slow death of the Earth.

Contempt

The Pierce brothers looked at each across the control console, one with contempt and hatred in his eyes, the other with fear and loathing.

'Henry ...' Harold began, but he couldn't find the words to continue.

The minute he'd seen his brother, he'd realized exactly what was happening. Banished from the Genesis 2 project all those years ago, Henry Pierce had had access to the data from the simulations, all the early planning and implementation of the project, and the Covenant. Which was why Zadra Nurmeen was at his side once again – it all made sense in an instant.

The delay with the lighting in Quadrant 1, the sabotaged neuronic devices, the hijacked shards ... everything that had gone wrong with this project so far had been down to his brother. And Zadra Nurmeen. Harold had believed that Zadra had been banished from Off World Federation business, but it was obvious that this evil pair had managed to stay in contact, working together all that time. But for what?

Harold Pierce looked at his brother. He had to be

stopped. Henry Pierce was pure, hyper-intelligent evil and although he'd learned to conceal it since his clumsy days as a young, spiteful child, he could never survive in the inner circle of the Genesis 2 project. Eventually the evil would break out and conquer his intellect, his rationality and his sense of right and wrong.

So it was with sadness and trepidation that Harold Pierce talked to his brother. As he began to speak, he understood that he would be forced to kill him – or he would be killed himself and the entire world put to death without mercy.

The Plan

Every detail had been considered in the Global Consortium's planning. It was important that the Quadrants could exist in open sight in these days of internet communication and satellite surveillance. They didn't want another Area 51 on their hands.

It had proven so easy to select the old military bunker facilities across the globe, then install the technology that would ultimately be used to deliver Genesis 2. While everybody had their eyes on the military big dogs like Cheyenne Mountain, work had been going on for many years on the four key installations that would support this global strategy. But it was what lay beneath the bunkers that would have created the biggest spark among the conspiracy theorists. Below each main bunker structure, work had begun many years ago to create vast underground containment areas for something that was not of this Earth.

Unknown to anybody else, other than the members of the Global Consortium, this work had involved off-world input, invoked as part of the Covenant which governed our planetary sector. Underneath each bunker, vast metal arks had been built. When the Consortium triggered Unification, these underground craft would be deployed to a task it had always been hoped would never be needed. Beneath each bunker was one part of a huge space ship, a Quadrant, which was capable of leaving Earth and docking together with the other three Quadrants to form one gigantic structure in space, thousands of miles above the planet. This structure was known as the Nexus.

As soon as Unification was initiated, the Quadrants would power up and emerge from their hiding places below ground, gliding out from the hillsides into which they'd been built and leaving the upper levels of the bunkers intact. The circular structure would be docked around the central hub, from which the Global Consortium would run this new world, as the perils that had struck the planet played out on the Earth below.

Each Quadrant had a specific purpose: for food, power, technology, and the creation of life itself. But Unification meant one thing, and it was only in the direst circumstances that it would be sanctioned by the Consortium. This was an evacuation of Earth.

Re-grouped

The shaking and vibration was prolonged and frightening. I was desperate for it to finish, but it continued for several minutes. It felt as if the whole place was about to collapse in on us. Cups and E-Pads were falling off the desks, and Mum told us to get underneath the large, solid conference table in the middle of the room in case the roof started to sustain some damage. Everybody in the briefing room was shaken by this, the room hushed. We were all fearful for our lives. Except Viktor, who remained cool and impassive. He appeared to have done this before.

Eventually the rumbling stopped and the stillness afterwards was wonderful. We all stayed quiet for a moment before emerging from under the table, as we gained confidence that it was over. We exited the briefing room and entered the control room where Magnus's team were shaken, but returning to their screens in the way they'd been trained to do.

A few minutes later we got a rundown on the latest data. What appeared to have happened was that Levels 3 and 4 had separated off and become airborne. A tech op posted a digital replay on the screen – we couldn't see the real thing because of the darkness outside the bunker, but we could see it digitized in front of us. The Quadrants all pieced together to create one vast structure, each part with its own function.

All the areas I'd seen so far – the embryos, the troops, the transporters, the weaponry, the drones – all those lower bunker levels in the different Quadrants had joined together to make one ship. That explained why the lower levels were so different. They were a separate structure entirely – they had a different purpose from the upper levels. It also made sense that they had their own operations centres, much better equipped than the upper-level control room we were in now.

So, what the heck was going on? We had a lot to take on board. Magnus took the initiative.

'We need to regroup, everybody – and fast!'

He issued a few commands to his staff – mainly to get more data about what had happened and what those four Quadrants were doing. He ushered us back into the briefing room and started to speak.

'Xiang, you need to gather a team and prioritize Dan and Nat's situation. Find out what accelerates and slows down the viral process, and look for a way to stop it.'

Xiang was already there. She'd been working at her E-Pad throughout the entire drama.

'Mike, you need to continue with the files analysis, focus on Dan and Nat, and see if you can find anything about what just happened with the lower levels.'

Dad was on the case. Everybody wanted to do something now – we were all fired up.

'I need to see Harriet and David,' interrupted Mum, 'but when I'm back, I want you to assign me a key task, Magnus. Don't keep me away from any of the good jobs.'

Mum's way of dealing with this was going to be to keep fighting. She wasn't going to lie down and watch things happen around her. Magnus told her to grab an assistant to guide her to the rec room where David and Harriet were being looked after. She rushed off. I'm embarrassed to say I'd forgotten my little brother and sister – they must have been terrified by what had happened. I was seeing a new side of Mum right now. She was pretty kick-ass, but she was still Mum – always concerned about the family, always making sure we were okay.

Magnus continued his regrouping exercise. This was his Quadrant and nobody challenged his authority.

'Viktor, you and I need to talk. I want to know more about these nukes of yours.'

Then he turned to me.

'Dan and Nat ...' he began. But Nat had gone.

Exit

Kate recognized Simon in an instant. Without the neuronic device in her neck, with a clear and fully conscious mind, she knew him the minute she saw him, in spite of his furtiveness.

'Simon! Why are you here?'

She knew that if Simon was in this place, at this time, with all that was going on, it must be linked to what had happened to the two of them in the past. She thought back to what they'd seen in that room before they were stunned by the lasers, whoever – or whatever – had been speaking to them during the botched military exercise. She knew immediately that it had to be connected.

Simon's hand moved to his weapon and he pointed it directly at her.

'Whoa!'

She held up her hands – as if that would have defended her.

'Steady, Simon. It's me Kate,' she continued, taken aback by his greeting. Simon ordered her to turn around and kneel down. Kate started to protest, but decided to do as she was told. She knew this man and supposed that he had a good reason for this. She didn't know what she'd done while under the control of Doctor Pierce, but she was beginning to get some rather worrying flashbacks. Holding the weapon to her head, he came in close and checked her neck.

'It worked,' he said after satisfying himself that Kate's neck implant was no longer active. 'Hell, Kate, you've caused some serious trouble here today. Are you aware of what's been going on?'

'No, I've no idea, Simon, but there's no time to talk. We need to get out of here. The troopers haven't yet figured out that I'm okay, but I reckon we only have a few minutes lead on them.'

The now repaired elevator arrived at its destination and Kate grabbed Simon's weapon and marched him out into the corridor. Level 3 was busy with trooper activity and she needed to make it look as if he was a captive. She took a deep breath as they started walking along the third level. She was still unchallenged, they weren't on to her just yet. They needed to use the transporter. She whispered to Simon.

'Where's safe?'

'Quadrant 3. That is, if you haven't taken it yet.'

'Not yet. We aborted when the disruption above ground began, luckily for you, Simon.'

'Lucky for both us!'

There was another violent tremor throughout the bunker, deep, sustained and penetrating.

'We need to leave!' he shouted. 'They've begun Unification.'

There was no time to talk. The troopers had automatically moved into a high alert status as soon as the rumbling had begun.

Kate and Simon strode confidently towards the transporter. But as she placed her hand on the console, its sym node providing the electronic signature needed to activate it, the troopers turned in unison to face her, weapons at the ready. They'd received a message from the Queen. They knew what Kate was doing.

They started to fire. Kate and Simon ducked behind the console.

'They've deactivated the sym node, Simon. We're trapped!'

CHAPTER THREE

The Covenant

The governments of the world had known of extra-terrestrial life for many years. Who could imagine we'd be allowed to leave our planet and send probes out into space without some form of intervention? As a species, we're so egocentric. Even though we know otherwise, we still see the universe in relation to ourselves, rather than the reality that the Earth is only a tiny speck in a much greater landscape.

When we began to prod the sleeping giant, it had to take action. An individual species would not be permitted to leave its own planet unchallenged, because of the repercussions that could happen elsewhere. So we were visited. Not in the form of flying saucers or little green men, as the conspiracy theorists might like us to believe. It was done discreetly. The systems of government had been studied from afar – it was quite clear how this would need to progress.

And so it was that the Global Consortium was formed

and Earth's leaders signed the Covenant, a binding agreement among intelligent species from twelve planets, outlining the rules of engagement, mutual support and information-sharing that would take place.

Referred to on Earth as the Off World Federation – or sometimes O-Fed for short – by the very few leaders who even knew of its existence, a yearly meeting would take place to discuss, revise and re-commit to the Covenant and to debate any outstanding issues. The meetings were held every 203 days – Federation time wasn't measured in Earth years – and the biggest topics of discussion for the past fifty-five years had been Earth's impending environmental doom and the mineral crisis that was going to destroy Helyios 4 only twenty years afterwards.

Gone

I needed to have words with Nat. She'd be no use to anybody if she kept disappearing like that. She was pretty angry about Doctor Pierce earlier and I hoped she hadn't gone rushing off to seek revenge on her own. I felt the same myself. With the minutes to my death counting down on my comms tab, I was just as keen as she was to solve this problem before our time was up. Two hours forty-six minutes to be precise.

Nat hadn't gone too far – I could still feel our connection, and she wouldn't be able to leave now without triggering the transporter alerts. Magnus had acted to secure the Quadrant against attack. We'd heard that Quadrants 2 and 4 – Viktor and Xiang's bunkers – had fallen to the troopers. Their teams managed to get word to us before they were rounded up and moved to the upper levels of their bunkers. They would probably be used as hostages, human pawns to be used to force our hand. They might not even have survived.

I shuddered at the thought of what might be going on in the other Quadrants. Before these events I'd never have said I was courageous, but right then, in the heat of the situation, I was feeling much bolder. I'd have a go at anything to fix this mess, but I was at a bit of a loss. What could I do? The adults were all away discussing things and hatching plans while I was left here waiting to self-terminate, or whatever it was Xiang said would happen. I was with Nat on this. I wasn't going to sit here waiting for the nanovirus to kill me.

The Custodians and adults could discuss their plans. I wasn't going to twiddle my thumbs while it all played out around me. I wished Nat had trusted me to come with her – I wanted in on this. I could feel that she was still in this bunker, and I was going to find her.

I was about to slip out of the control room when the alert sirens sounded. Somebody – or something – had breached the transporters.

Rescue

While everybody had been regrouping, Nat was the only one to notice Simon trying to get attention via the comms tab. He was in some serious trouble – she could hear weapon fire as he tried to speak to her and tell her what was going on. She was certain he was with somebody, but she couldn't tell who it was.

The sym nodes had been deactivated and so he would

need one of the twins to operate the transporter. That meant Dan or herself. Dan was at the other side of the room and she couldn't attract his attention without making a big deal of it, so she would have to do it. She slipped out of the control room, along the corridor and to the elevator.

Nat hadn't a clue what would happen now the upper and lower levels of the bunker had been separated. She assumed that Levels 3 and 4 would just be some vast, empty hangar area.

There was no time to experiment – she needed to use her genetic advantage to save Simon. Although the sym nodes had been disabled, she was certain that everything would still work for her and Dan, and she was right. Nat was able to activate the upper buttons in the elevator. As she stared at the strange symbols placed above the level numbering, she hoped she'd got the right combination to take her to where she needed to be. This was going to be a delicate operation.

Simon was still live on her comms tab. It was looking desperate for him and his companion.

'Coming now!' she cried.

The elevator began its metamorphosis and in a matter of seconds Nat appeared on a transporter platform just behind Simon in Quadrant 1. All around them weapons were being fired, and there was an explosion just to her right as she materialized in the room. She could feel that this Quadrant was moving – it felt like being in a huge aeroplane. The transporters were still working even though the upper and lower Quadrants had become separated.

'Simon, run!' she yelled.

Simon and his companion kept their heads down and ran as fast as they could. Simon fired randomly behind him to discourage the troopers from taking an open shot at him.

As he and Kate made it to the transporter, Nat activated the console and they began to dematerialize. But in the panic and weaponry fire, Nat pressed the fifth button by mistake, the one that had appeared across the entire transporter network at the moment Unification was initiated.

They'd escaped the immediate danger of the troopers, but they hadn't made it back to the bunker. As they exited the transporter, they stepped out into a curved corridor. Nat didn't look back to see who Simon's companion was, she was immediately distracted by this new place. It was lined with windows. She looked outside to get a sense of where she was. They weren't in a bunker, they were in space.

CHAPTER FOUR

14 April 1990

The business of the Off World Federation had gone on since the 1940s, unknown to the majority of the world's leaders. Initially contact was restricted to those countries with the capacity to send rockets, animals and – eventually – people into space. Off World Federation members were bound to strict rules.

Each of the twelve planets which formed this alliance were at different stages in their evolution. Some were advanced technologically, others lived simple lives and were concerned more with cerebral matters. One planet, Zatheon, resembled Earth. It was dominated by humanoid and intelligent life forms but advanced in terms of its technology, social justice and environmental initiatives. In fact, Zatheon was not dissimilar to a utopian version of the Earth that science fiction writers might create, an evolved version of the planet where petty squabbles between leaders were largely resolved, democracy was universally applied, and a fair but firm justice system permitted the inhabitants to live a high quality of life.

As a consequence of each planet's unique circumstances, there were binding rules for Off World Federation members. These rules included allowing other planets to co-exist with no external interference, to preserve life on any planet that was under threat, and to restrict space travel, exploration and exploitation of other uninhabited planets to agreed zones.

One of the rules enshrined in this interplanetary pact related to the level of contact permitted between planets. Only a very limited number of leaders on each planet knew about the Off World Federation. For the general population, life on other planets was largely a matter of conjecture and rumour. But the issues on Helyios 4 and Earth had resulted in a new pact, an agreement for three planets to share expertise and data.

When the Global Consortium was formed in 1983, compelling the divided nations across the globe to work together to solve the looming environmental catastrophe, it followed shortly afterwards that any solution must also involve off-world input. It was sanctioned by the Off World Federation because it pertained to preserving life and keeping two member planets alive, an overarching principle of this alliance. And so O-Fed became involved in the Genesis 2 project. There was an agreement that technology and expertise could be shared, but it must be used and contained only in this project, it was not to be deployed to accelerate progress and technological advances elsewhere on Earth.

Helyios 4 was also granted this privilege. The problems

facing that planet were mineral based. Their power sources were becoming completely depleted. The Helyions were a formidable and warlike people who lived predominantly underground. They thrived in radioactive environments, their industry was heavy and destructive, and they were a disruptive force within the Off World Federation.

There was a feeling among the more advanced planets that Helyios 4 needed to become part of the inner circle or – in many generations' time, when their ability to travel deep into space had evolved – they might be inclined to play the role of aggressor. The Off World Federation felt it was better to guide and influence rather than to leave the planet to its own devices and the inevitable violent conclusion.

It was because of these pacts that Zadra Nurmeen had been permitted to leave Helyios 4 to work alongside the humans on Earth. And it was the reason that a female mineral specialist was sent to the same planet, as an emissary from Zatheon – a gifted mineralogist who was to end up years later as the tortured captive of the Helyions that she was supposed to be helping.

The Fifth Button

The control room was on red alert. Magnus had rushed away from whatever he and Viktor were discussing to attend to the breach.

Since the Quadrants had separated, the main vulnerability seemed to be via the elevators on Levels 1 and 2. The transporter areas on the lower levels were now hovering above the planet – they'd broken away from the main bunker. Security in the elevator areas was tight, and there were heavily armed guards on both levels. The screens in the control room were switched to multi-camera view so Magnus could see the nature of the breach. It had come in on Level 1, the floor above us, and the tension in the room was high. The doors hadn't yet opened. We watched and waited. There was complete silence.

As the doors began to open some kind of probe flew fast out of them, making those of us watching on the screens jump. Immediately came shots from the security teams and the probe exploded, falling to the ground.

'They're preparing to take over the Quadrants,' Magnus announced. 'They're checking out our defences first.'

The security chief who had overseen the shooting down of the probe spoke over the comms system.

'It's a 360-degree probe. They just got a complete feed of our fortifications. I'd recommend that we disable the transporters.'

Magnus wasn't so sure – I could see it in his face. He knew, like everybody else in the room, that if we blew up the elevators we could prevent a trooper attack, but in doing so we'd abandon the bunker teams who'd been captured in the other three Quadrants. I reckoned Viktor and Xiang wouldn't go for that either.

Magnus made his choice – we were going for defence, but he still ordered the security teams to wire the elevators with explosives. If they had to be destroyed, they could be, at the push of a button. But for the meantime they were our portals to the remaining Quadrants and they needed to be defended. Magnus gave instructions to deploy additional security, effectively creating levels of deterrence three lines deep along each stretch of corridor opening to the elevators.

My comms tab beeped. It was Nat – at last. One look at her face told me I needed to take this message on my own.

I sneaked into one of the smaller meeting rooms. I had to know what she was up to.

'Nat, where are you?'

The video feed from her tab blurred momentarily, then adjusted on her view. It took my eyes a second to refocus – surely I wasn't really seeing what I thought that was? Another blur as she repositioned the comms tab so I could see her face again.

'I'm in space, Dan. It's amazing!'

'How the heck did you get there?'

I was incredulous. This had started out as a family day trip – nobody mentioned space travel.

'Dan, there's a new button on the transporters. It seems to have appeared after the Quadrants separated. I pressed it by accident and we've surfaced somewhere in space. We're on some kind of space station. You need to join us, but keep it quiet for now, I don't know how it fits in with things yet.'

I was desperate to join Nat. Surely this must be the hub for what was going on. It would make perfect sense bearing in mind how the Quadrants had separated and started to move above the surface of the planet. Nat and I had the run of the place. Nobody was challenging us or treating us like kids – there was a general understanding that we were key to everything.

I think it had finally sunk in for me too. At first it had seemed unbelievable that any of this could be connected with me. But seeing what I'd seen in those bunkers over the past forty-eight hours, being reunited with a twin I thought was dead, finding out that my mum and dad had lived hidden lives which they hadn't cared to share with us. It was just incredible.

I was getting the hang of it now, and I liked it. When I was in the bunker entrance after the darkness fell, I was scared, fearful, a victim. Not any more. I was energized, motivated and angry. I wanted to fix this thing, and now I could see where Nat's anger was coming from.

I wasn't going to be a victim. I was getting off my butt to sort this or I'd die trying.

So I checked out with Nat and told her to wait. I was on my way ... to space!

A New Ally

As Nat switched off her comms tab, she turned away from the window looking out onto the stars and registered for the first time who her second companion had been.

'Hell! Kate!'

She launched herself at her, enraged. Simon was fast to intervene. It was a good job too – Nat hit him with quite some force.

'Hold on, Nat!'

He was struggling to restrain her. Nat could see that Kate was taken aback by her attack, but she was only prepared to give Simon thirty seconds to come up with a good reason why she shouldn't continue. As it was, Kate started to explain. She hadn't met Nat yet, but she could tell already that she was extremely spirited.

'Nat, you're fine. I'm not a threat to you.'

Nat smouldered and didn't look convinced. Kate picked up quickly. She liked this young woman and could see something of her own fire in her. Simon felt the tension in Nat's arms ease slightly, so he offered some reassurance.

'It's okay, Nat. Kate and I know each other from way back.'

Nat showed she was ready to listen, but only for a short time.

'I can't explain what happened to me in the bunker,' said Kate. 'I knew what I was doing, but somehow it didn't concern me, I seemed to have lost my free will. I can only describe it as if someone was controlling me. My conscience had disappeared, it didn't seem to matter. But when the explosion went off on the surface, something happened – it was as if I'd got my senses back. I knew that what I'd done wasn't good. I took one look around the control room and the troopers, and I got out of there fast.'

Nat was interested now. Simon gave Kate a bit more help.

'It's these devices in their necks, Nat, the same as your mum and James have ...'

He hesitated at the mention of James.

'Kate was being controlled for most of the time she was in Quadrant 1.'

'We need to find out who's doing this, Nat,' Kate continued, 'and I'll bet any amount of money the answer lies right here!'

They'd all come to the same conclusion at the same time. You didn't need to be a detective to figure it out. Whatever answers they were after would be found here. And all three wanted to speak to one man in particular. Doctor Pierce was the key to this. As they stood there in that corridor in space, a new alliance formed in an instant and became glued by mutual contempt for the same man.

Suddenly the lights went out. The entire structure powered down then rebooted. It took less than a minute, but it was obvious that something important had just happened.

A voice, cold, without emotion, almost robotic came through the speakers which lined the corridor. It was a female voice, but one which sounded detached, as if all humanity had been washed away and discarded.

'Your Queen has taken control of the Nexus. The final assault on Earth can now begin.'

CHAPTER FIVE

Emissary From Helyios 4

On 10 July 1999 a 32-year-old mineralogist from the planet Zatheon began a unique placement on Earth. This was only the second time one of her species had been to the planet, and she was privileged and honoured to have been chosen for the task.

Even at such a young age, Davran Saloor was highly proficient in her field. She was the leading expert in mineralogy on her home planet, surpassing the skills of her own mentor and teacher and making ground-breaking discoveries about mineral composition that revolutionized all thinking and learning on the topic.

So, when the Off World Federation finally heard the pleas from Helyios 4 to assist with the mineral depletions that would eventually kill their own planet, the elders on Zatheon thought it only fit to send Davran to Earth. That planet had a very similar mineral composition to Helyios 4, so Davran's task was to apply the knowledge and principles developed on her own planet to see how they might help with the crisis.

Davran was also crucial to Earth's own terraforming proposals. They would use technology from her own planet Zatheon to facilitate this process and deploy lessons learned in the resurrection of Helyios 4 when their turn came. Accompanying her would be the abrupt and rude Zadra Nurmeen, who had been dispatched from Helyios 4 to work alongside two prominent scientists from Earth, both of them at the forefront of Earth's Genesis 2 project.

These unprecedented steps for off-world species to interact with each other were subject to draconian controls. Under no circumstances would the Off World Federation permit contact with other humans not directly engaged in the respective projects of Earth and Helyios 4.

Although Davran was humanoid in appearance, her biological make-up was very different to that of the humans. Her skin was light, her hair dark and her eyes a piercing grey, but there was nothing about her – other than her manner, habits and slight difficulty making the 'th' sound in human words – that would have given her away on Earth.

Zadra was also predominantly humanoid in form, but it was absolutely imperative that he was not seen, as his eyes, nose shape and skin texture would have made him stand out immediately among human beings. His species was well adapted to hard physical work so they tended to be short and compact. On each hand they had seven fingers for more effective use of tools in tight underground locations.

Zadra and Davran, along with the twin scientists from Earth, were well aware of the consequences of breaching the code of engagement agreed by the members of the Off World Federation. No contact with humans unless they'd been given full Genesis 2 clearance. No tests, experiments or processes to be carried out unless within the agreed remits and specifications. A complete and total confidentiality clause on all off-planet experiences. These rules were crucial to the integrity and peaceful co-existence of the twelve planets which formed the Off World Federation.

Which is why, when she breached the code, Davran was subjected to such severe and terrible consequences.

Supremacy

For a sociopath like Henry Pierce, throwing his own brother violently from his chair at the helm of the control console was a spiteful and long overdue victory. One which he had imagined now for many years, and one which he knew he'd savour when the opportunity finally came.

The Off World Federation could come up with as many rules and codes as it liked, but when Doctor Henry Pierce and Zadra Nurmeen had met, there had been an instant ignition of friendship, one which would have no respect for those rules. As Henry learned more about Helyios 4, he began to feel that he'd been born on the wrong planet and at the wrong time. He had much more in common with the values of his new friend. So when Henry and Zadra narrowly escaped ostracism after their own debacles, the bond had already been forged. Two hate-filled men with a mission for revenge against a perceived enemy which had been merciful in its treatment of these offenders.

But they had knowledge, they'd been exposed to the far-reaching plans which affected both of their planets. And the woman from Zatheon had been the one to give them the key. Helyios 4 needed minerals, minerals which were in plentiful supply on Earth. Henry Pierce hated Earth – they'd rejected him and failed to appreciate his skills and intelligence. Earth was dying and Genesis 2 was going to save it. But using the knowledge and expertise of the mineralogist from Zatheon, as well as the privileged access Pierce and Nurmeen had had before being taken off the project, it was possible to sabotage Genesis 2.

Henry Pierce's aims were simple. They didn't take any account of interplanetary codes or off-world covenants. Henry Pierce cared only about himself. With his friend Zadra Nurmeen he would destroy his brother's work. He would then sabotage the Genesis 2 project. The Earth would be destroyed – a failed mission, an Off World Federation project gone sadly wrong. Under Federation laws, if Earth died of its own accord, its mineral deposits were fair game, where no sentient or intelligent life existed – or was capable of existing. They'd make sure of that. The shards were already injecting the poisons that would kill this planet. Earth had begun to burn. Henry and Zadra would become vastly rich and powerful selling the mineral supplies back to Helyios 4. Henry would return to that planet as its saviour. This dream was within his grasp.

As Harold fell to the floor, he kicked him with the contempt he thought he deserved. Blood began to trickle from his mouth and head, and Henry was reminded of the delightful time he'd enjoyed when he'd poured scalding hot water over his brother as they'd bathed when children.

He keyed in some codes on the control panel before him. The power went off momentarily, then resumed. It was not unlike what had happened in the bunkers hours earlier, only without the twenty-four hour delay that had been necessary to infiltrate the Global Consortium mainframe. That was when they were most vulnerable, at the point at which power was handed over from world governments to his brother.

A cold female voice came over the speaker system in the ops area. The Queen was connected to the Nexus. Harold Pierce would be eliminated and the final processes to kill off the Earth could at last be put in place. With the Queen now online, the troopers would quickly overcome and destroy the final bunker.

Having recovered slightly from the violence of Henry's attack, Harold Pierce began to pick himself off the floor. He should have stayed where he was. Henry kicked him once again, hard and ruthlessly in the head. Harold dropped, unconscious, bruised and bloody. Henry sneered at him. The brothers looked so alike he could be watching himself lying there, pathetic, on the floor. Only he would never let anybody do that to him. Life to him was about supremacy, dominance, victory. Right now, in this moment, he felt indestructible. With his friend Zadra Nurmeen at his side, he would destroy the cursed planet thousands of kilometres below them and live a new life on Helyios 4 where he would be rich, adored and powerful. And he would achieve it using the skills of another person who'd been cast aside, just like he was all those years ago. It was good to hear her voice in the ops area at last – the final part of this plan was coming together, after so many years.

She would be his secret weapon, it would be her power that would allow him to make the final twist of the knife and kill the planet he hated so much.

Breakthrough

. . .

Amy sidled up to Mike, who was working furiously at his console. Both knew how important these events were – they had just over two hours to save Nat and Dan.

Amy felt helpless. She didn't have Mike's ability with the tech, there was nothing special about her DNA, she hadn't been gifted with Xiang's expertise or skills, or Viktor's military prowess. She'd seen Harriet and David. They were having a great time in the rec room – the bunker staff were taking excellent care of them. She felt redundant. None of the kids seemed to need her. And then there was Nat, who had come back from the dead. Amy just wanted to hold her once again, but even Nat's thoughts were elsewhere, just like Dan's. She had to accept that the twins were both adults now.

She and Mike had been so proud when the adoption had been given the go-ahead, when the beautiful twins had been handed over to them at three years old. Now they were on their way in the world. She was immensely impressed by what they'd done over the past forty-eight hours, but she was also filled with sadness. Amy knew that after this she'd never have her two young kids back again – they were grown up now. Even Mike was distracted. She knew why – he was busy – busy trying to save their children.

Then she got it. There was still somebody who needed her. James had been all but abandoned. Sure, they were trying to figure out what had happened to him. But what if he was wounded, or needed some help? Amy wasn't going to sit around doing nothing. Somebody needed her still, it was her friend Roachie, he would be glad to see her.

So she kissed Mike and headed back out to the control room, where she met Dan who had just left one of the meeting rooms. Okay, he might have been growing up, but she could still see it all over his face. He was up to something. And she was coming too.

Separate Missions

As I was making my exit from the control room I ran into Mum. Her timing could have been better.

Where are you going, Dan?

Er, space, Mum.

Remember to phone me when you get there.

As if that was how it was going to work out.

'Where are you going, Dan? You look like you're up to something.'

Darn, she knew everything. Still, there was no way I was telling her where I was heading.

She put her arm around me. My instinct was to pull away, but I let her have this one. Me and Nat could be dead in a couple of hours. Of course she was worried. I thought she was going to pump me for more information, but then I got a surprise. She told me what she was planning and I ended up being the one to tell her to be careful. She was heading for the elevator, same as me, but she was going to Quadrant 1 – she had her sym node activated and a weapon in her hand.

I couldn't really get all protective about Mum saving James when I was about to join Nat in space to save my own skin. It seemed so ridiculous and unreal. We'd have to press pause on normal life until this was over. It made me laugh to myself just thinking about how preposterous it sounded. Dan Tracy, spaceman. The whole thing was crazy.

Nobody challenged us as we headed for the elevator,

although we had to wait for the man wiring the explosives around the door. Once inside, we saw there were explosives in there too.

'Are we okay to use this?' I asked. It looked a bit serious to me.

'You're good to go,' the explosives guy replied. 'We'll only blow this if they send troopers over. When you come back, alert us via your comms tabs – you've got about two seconds after those doors open. If we think you're troopers or if we get a glimpse of troopers, we blow it.'

Nice to know. I'd try not to look like a trooper when I came back.

Nobody even challenged us about where we were going or why. Magnus was giving us the run of the place. With just over two hours to live and the destruction of the planet already in motion, I guessed there was only so much damage a sixteen-year-old kid could do.

Nat was right about the elevator. An illuminated panel had appeared above the weird symbols we'd used to get to the other bunkers. Mum pressed the symbol to get her to Quadrant 1 but nothing happened. She tried a few other options but there was nothing. The sym node must be broken – or even worse, deactivated. That would make sense. If Kate realized we were able to use these things, she'd block us immediately. Just like Dad had when he found me logging into his social media accounts and writing daft messages.

Before I pressed the button a hunch made me grab one of the explosives packs that had been secured around the elevator. The explosives wouldn't transport with us – it didn't seem to work that way, so I needed to pick them up and carry them. I did the honours with the buttons, and it all worked fine for me. After all, I was the kid with the special genes. The same genes that were going to kill me in a couple of hours.

The light display flashed to show that we were being transported. I took Mum back to the upper level in Quadrant 1. Before opening the doors we paused to look at each other. I drew the weapon I had tucked away in my pocket from our earlier gunfight. We both nodded and then I pressed the button to open the doors. We took a side each. I couldn't believe our luck. There were two troopers, one on either side, and we incapacitated them straight away. That was a bit too easy. Perhaps they thought they had us on the run and never expected us to make our way back there.

Mum gave me a massive hug, the kind of hug you give somebody if it might be the last time you're going to see them.

'I love you, Dan ... and I'm so proud of you.'

'I love you too, Mum. Kick some butt and make sure you get back alright. How can me and Nat get killed by a nanovirus if you're not even around to say goodbye?'

She was tearful but I'd managed to make her laugh. She gave my arm a final squeeze.

The black lights in the necks of the incapacitated troopers were pulsating furiously – we had a good idea what that meant. We'd just stuck our hands in a hornet's nest. We didn't have the weapons set to kill, we'd only stunned them. It was an effective stun though, it seemed to last for at least an hour. I might have been threatened with death myself but I didn't want to kill anyone. Not yet at least. Despite their menacing appearance we had to remember the troopers were human underneath. Sure, they seemed to have it in for us, but they may have been as responsible for their actions as Mum and James were earlier. If I could avoid a kill, I would, so long as it didn't put our lives at risk.

Mum rushed up the corridor. She grabbed one of the trooper's weapons and a helmet for good measure. She was thinking of the darkness beyond the bunker doors, I reckoned – maybe she didn't trust that thing in her neck which had seemed to protect her before. Within seconds she'd disappeared. I could hear movement along the corridors. They were on to her already. I had a bright idea, but I wasn't sure it would work. I placed the explosives I'd transported with us about a hundred metres along the corridor, in the opposite direction to Mum. That's all I dared to do. I could hear the thudding boots of the troopers approaching at speed.

I ran back to the elevator, took cover inside with the doors still open, then fired at the explosives. Two shots, three shots, then another. Darn, I kept missing. I was a lousy shot. I ran out again into the corridor and got ready to fire again. I had no idea how powerful the stuff was. Surely it wouldn't make too much of a bang? As the first trooper appeared along the corridor, I shot again. This time I hit my target, but it didn't explode. One more try. I changed the settings on my weapon to kill, fired again and missed. Laser fire streaked past my head. The troopers were trying to kill me. I'd fire one last time, but then I'd have to run. I squeezed the trigger.

The explosion was huge. What had I done? I was thrown right back and it took me a few minutes to come round. I was stunned by the noise and violence of what had just happened. My ears were ringing. Dust and debris were everywhere. I couldn't see any troopers and their weaponry fire had stopped, for now at least. I picked myself off the floor, ran into the elevator and pressed the new button. The fifth button.

That must have bought Mum some time. If she could

get to James, the two of them would be able to work together to make it back to Quadrant 3. Or they could just sit it out until this was all over. However it ended.

As before, the elevator dissolved into an array of lights and the transportation was underway. I couldn't feel anything, I was only aware of being in a brightly lit grid which, as if by magic, was moving me from one place to another thousands of kilometres away. Out into space.

Before the door opened I took a deep breath, much like you do if you've travelled to the top of a very tall building, collecting your thoughts while you brace yourself for what lies ahead. I opened the doors, ready to see Nat. But as I stepped out into the corridor, I walked straight into a firestorm.

CHAPTER SIX

Collusion

Magnus had been quick to work out the type of man Viktor was. He was an astute judge of character and he saw an intelligence, cunning and potential for violence in Viktor which he did not possess himself.

Magnus was at heart an entrepreneur, a man with an amazing vision for technology and the ability to assemble a team with talents far greater than his own and thus make great things happen. In Viktor he saw an opportunity, a chance to connect with somebody who might help this entire situation play out in a different way. Like all of the Custodians in the Quadrants, he was largely blind to what was going on. Bit by bit, snippets of information were emerging, but it was not even clear yet who the enemy was, or how powerful they might be. So Magnus was making contingency plans.

He would never have mentioned it in front of Mike,

Amy or the kids, but the chances of Dan and Nat getting out of this situation alive were pretty slim. Xiang had had to relocate her laboratory set-up to Quadrant 3, effectively starting again, except for the full data compilation which she'd brought with her on her E-Pad. Magnus's team was made up of brilliant people, but in his Quadrant they'd been assembled on the basis of their technical abilities, not their experiences in the field of biology, as with the Beijing Quadrant. So it was unlikely that Dan and Nat were getting out of this in one piece, and Magnus saw in Viktor's eyes that he understood this too.

The steps they'd taken to protect against a trooper assault would hold off an attack for now, but it would only delay it in the short term, and eventually this Quadrant would be overrun just like the others. Who knew what would happen to the bunker personnel? Those poor souls unlucky enough to be caught in the other Quadrants would already be confronting their fate at the hands of the enemy.

Magnus knew he needed another plan, a final option – the nuclear option. To his knowledge, with the limited information he had at his fingertips, Quadrant 3 was where the last stand would be made. He had already sanctioned the launch of Viktor's nuclear subs along with Xiang earlier, but now it was time to arm them and set in some targets. Just in case.

So, when Viktor and Magnus quietly sidled off into a meeting room, they were not discussing how Viktor might contribute to the work being done in Quadrant 3, as everybody else might have thought. They were actually discussing targets for the biggest nuclear assault that the world had ever seen.

. . .

Lab Tests

Xiang was frustrated. She'd made excellent progress so far, but now she was no longer able to access her lab facilities and she was struggling. She looked at the readings on her E-Pad. Nat's progress through the nanovirus process was at 71 percent, Dan seemed to be accelerating at 44 percent. She would keep working until the final moment, but she had a strong feeling that the twins weren't going to make it. She was weighed down by the responsibility on her shoulders. She held the lives of these two teenagers in her hands, yet she seemed to have so little chance of saving them in the ridiculously tight timescale she had to work with.

She felt alone and isolated. Magnus had assigned her a team, but these people were not specialists in her field. She needed people who could keep up with her, who might even be ahead of her at times. She was overcome by a surge of concern and sadness for the people she'd left back in Beijing. Communications had been cut as soon as the troopers had breached their transporters. She didn't know how many of the mobile masts had been disabled, what damage the drones had done to her city, and what terrible things might be happening to her colleagues.

Xiang shuddered, then focused her mind on the task in hand. This situation would have to play out – there were forces at work here, over which she had no influence. Other people were dealing with security matters. That was not her main area of expertise. She understood that the greatest contribution she could possibly make to this crisis would be to save the twins. At any cost. They were pivotal to this entire scenario. They weren't moping around waiting to die.

They were fighting, and that's what Xiang would do. She would play this change in circumstances to her advantage. Her new team were not biological experts, but that meant they had unique and differing perspectives. And that's just what she needed right now, fresh pairs of eyes on a tricky problem.

Xiang steeled herself for the most important two hours of her life. That was the time she had left to save these two important youngsters: twins in whose hands the key to this terrible situation appeared to be held. She would flip this on its head – look at it from another angle. If she couldn't fix the twins in time, how could she circumnavigate it? What if she could find somebody like the twins, with the same genetic make-up? A transfusion of blood might be possible, it might buy her some time to figure out how to save them.

This thing had been done to Dan and Nat – in fact something had been done initially to Nat to trigger the process. If something can be done, it can be undone. She'd need some tech to do this. This was a nanovirus, created with microtechnology and biological processes. It would not take a regular transfusion or medical procedure, but she had a room full of tech ops to help her. She could do this – she was certain she could. She'd do the biology, they could manage the nanotech element.

If only she had the missing piece, somebody with the same genetic make-up as the twins.

Hidden Folders

Mike felt guilty that he'd barely acknowledged Amy and

now she was off, who knew where? He was so focused on the task in hand – he needed to start breaking into these files and getting some answers.

Dan and Nat had about two hours left by his reckoning. Xiang was working on it, he knew that, but if he could only break into those damn folders he'd be able to shortcut a lot of the learning processes and get directly to some answers.

Mike was feeling his age. Sure, all of this stuff followed consistent principles that had been in place since he was a teenage hacker himself, but things change and he was having to figure them out as he went along. It felt like the team that Magnus had assigned to help him were streets ahead of him. Only they'd never hacked, they'd been the kind of geeks who'd created the systems Mike had broken into all those years ago.

He had to spin his mind around and adopt another approach, this was taking too long. Then he saw it – it had been there all the time, right in front of him. He was looking for something that wasn't there, and it was why all these young techs surrounding him couldn't see it either. These files were old school. Whoever had set up these systems must be his age or older. They'd made the whole system more secure by playing the younger geeks at their own game. Clever. Very clever. He'd missed it at first. All the young coders thought they were so cool with their hacking and amazing scripts. They'd have a good laugh at MS-DOS, CP/M and TSR routines, but they didn't know these systems, they regarded them as prehistoric.

So the best way to cheat the youngest, best and fastest coders? Go retro, they'd never expect it. They'd be looking for all the latest whizz-bang encryption techniques when right under their noses you'd gone flashback. Sure, there was some modern stuff in there to throw them off the scent, but Mike had it now, he could see it clear as day. It was like being sixteen years old again. This security was a nod back to the good old days when only a handful of geeks were hacking in their spare time, rather than it being an actual category at the job centre as it seemed to be these days.

Mike put his theory to the test. He was in, he was right. One by one, the folders unlocked. Mike had opened up the heart of the Genesis 2 project. And now he was able to peer inside and find out what made it beat.

Captured

A red ray narrowly missed my head as I stepped out of the transporter door. The windows opposite confirmed that I was in the right place – I could see stars and blackness, just like Nat said.

There was no time to gawp. I'd obviously walked into something I shouldn't have. I wished I'd taken more explosives with me, although I wasn't sure I was ready to chance an explosion in space. A solid concrete bunker on Earth was about the limit of my risk-taking.

'Dan, is that you?'

It was Nat, her voice coming from around the corner. I could hear her returning weapon fire – I didn't dare to step out into the corridor. It was noisy and dangerous out there.

'Yes, it's me, Nat. What's going on?' I yelled.

'They've started to fill this place with troopers. It happened just after we heard the weird voice over the speakers. This is the centre of it all—'

I could hear her cursing.

'You okay, Nat?'

'Yes, I think so. I almost got hit by a laser ray. I'm with Simon and Kate. They're going to help me give you cover.'

Kate? Did anything stay the same here for more than five minutes?

'What's Kate doing here? Have you captured her?'

This was the woman who'd launched all the drones. I wasn't sure I was ready to be besties just yet.

'I'll explain later, Dan. But she's one of us, it's okay. We're going to cover you. You need to turn right out of the elevator.

'After three, Dan ... 3-2-1... *now!*'

I ran out of the elevator, turning right and landing in the middle of a blaze of laser fire. All around me were violent explosions as rays of light hit the walls, the ceiling and the floor.

'You mean *your* right, Nat!' I shouted, realizing I'd turned the wrong way out of the doors. I was running straight at the troopers. I could see them there: black, strong, formidable. You've never seen such a fast direction change. In fact, I don't think I've ever done something quite so athletic in my entire life.

Simon, Kate and Nat started a constant blast of fire in the direction of the troopers – I couldn't believe that none of those deadly rays had hit me yet. I wondered whether they were actually trying to kill me, but this was no time to compile a FAQ. I turned and dived in a way I would never have dreamed I was capable of before. As I landed near Simon's feet, I rolled and took cover around the corner, well out of the way of the red rays. I was breathless, but relieved, and just a little bit impressed with myself. I wished I could have rustled up some of those moves while my PE teacher at school was advising me to spend less time at my PC and more time kicking a football around outdoors.

'We'll give them everything we've got, then run!' Simon shouted.

'Shouldn't we escape in the transporter?' I suggested, but I was overruled by Kate, of all people.

'No, Dan, this is where this thing ends. We need to be on board whatever this spaceship is, this is where we'll get our answers.'

It made sense. With two hours left to live, Nat and I needed to run towards this problem, not away from it. And if we were hit in the heat of battle? Well, we were both goners in two hours anyway. I glanced at the feed Xiang had added to my comms tab. My nanovirus level was at 49 percent – how had it gone up so fast and so suddenly? Adrenalin, maybe. I hoped Xiang was working away in Quadrant 3. She was going to need to pull a rabbit out of a hat. And very soon too, by the look of it.

'We need to separate, guys,' said Simon. 'We stand more chance of making progress if we split off. I'll go with Kate and you need to stick together, Dan and Nat. Make sure you keep checking in with Magnus. They need to know where you are if they make a breakthrough.'

He was talking sense. We couldn't just disappear – if Xiang discovered a cure for the nanovirus we needed to be back in Quadrant 3.

'We'll take the left fork, you take the right one,' said Kate. I was finding it difficult to place my trust in her, but I couldn't see any life in her neck device right then, so I had to follow Simon and Nat's cue.

'Are we all connected via comms tabs?' asked Simon, and we checked our devices. Whatever technology these things used, it seemed to work fine up there. The same with the transporters. It was clear that all of this was linked up. The space station could just as easily have been part of a bunker. It looked exactly the same.

There was a massive thud and the entire structure shook. It was similar to the feeling I had when the lower Quadrant sections began to move when we were in the bunker. It was a deep, thunderous, violent tremor. I glanced outside the windows and looking below I could see what was happening. The four Quadrants had made their journey from Earth to space. They were docking with the space station, and that was what was causing the shaking. It had stopped the weapon fire for a moment, at least. It must have caught the troopers by surprise too.

'Run! Now!' Kate suddenly commanded. She was the first to gather her wits. We all fired a few random shots up the corridor towards the troopers, then each group took its agreed fork in the corridor.

We were going deep into the heart of the place now. The windows were gone and we could just be in one of the other bunkers, as far as I was concerned. The shaking had stopped. I counted four great thuds – that had to be all of the Quadrants docked.

The structure must have been huge. The upper levels of our Scottish bunker were supposed to be the size of a couple of football pitches while the vast lower levels spread out over a much greater area, so I couldn't imagine how big the place was now.

Simon and Kate were off. It seemed they'd done this sort of thing before – they were a team.

I looked at Nat.

'You okay?' I asked. It seemed that everything had been crazy for the past few days. We'd barely had time to speak.

'Yeah. I'm just thinking of the time. We haven't got long left.'

'We'll talk later, but let's finish this thing now, however it ends for us.'

Before she could answer, a green laser ray hit her chest and she slumped to the ground. For a split second I was aware of a sickening rush of fear, then a second ray hit me too. It was over.

CHAPTER SEVEN

Lost Friend

Amy heard an explosion along the corridor. She stopped for a moment, fearful for Dan, but then ran on. She was seeing a different side of her son and she knew she'd have to trust him. He'd played enough of those blasted computer games in his life to have every bit as much idea of military strategy as she did. Her guess was that he'd detonated those explosives in the corridor to slow down the troopers. Good call, Dan, and thanks for the head start.

She made her way up the corridor, where only days before she and her family had explored a dusty old cold-war bunker. How she yearned to be back there right now, to those safe, carefree family days before the darkness fell. Away from attacking troopers and drone bombardments, shoot-outs and medical crises. She'd walked away from this life at the age of nineteen when she left the army, and never looked back. Those events with James had been quite enough for her, she'd long ago decided that a life of dramatic excitement was not for her.

She neared the blast door area where she'd been reunited with James hours earlier. She looked towards the end of the corridor. The doors were open, the shimmering lights were acting as a barrier between the bunker and the darkness outside. There was a solitary guard there. The team they'd sent to retrieve Roachie must still have been out there.

She put on the helmet she'd taken from the trooper earlier. She cursed that it was no longer possible to pass herself off as regular bunker staff. When she first entered this place with Nat all she'd needed was a pair of overalls and a name badge. That reminded her, her laptop was still in the dorm area with James's blood on it where she'd whacked him on the head. Poor guy, he'd been through a lot.

The helmet took a little getting used to, but having already spent twenty-four hours in the darkness beyond the doors, Amy knew what was out there and understood this would require some assistance. Wearing the helmet and carrying the weapon she'd retrieved from the trooper, she was hoping she'd be able to make it quite some way up the corridor before the guard realized something was wrong. With the initiative hers, she reckoned she'd be able to stun him before she was spotted. It was worth a try anyway. She was just bracing herself and summoning up the courage to start the long walk up the corridor when there was a commotion at the blast doors.

A group of troopers stepped out of the darkness, through the shimmering wall of lights, back into the bunker entrance. They'd been alerted by the Queen. The minute Dan had set off the explosives deep within the bunker, the troopers had been diverted from their task of chasing James on the surface high above. Their mission was to find and terminate whoever had entered the bunker, before they could get back to the elevator and escape.

Amy was quick to realize what this meant, but she could just about see from that distance that the troopers were carrying something – or someone. She hesitated, thinking through her options. Her only way out was via the elevator transporter, but even then she wasn't sure if she could activate it anymore with the sym node no longer working.

She needed to resolve the issue with Roachie. Did he need help? There were only six troopers in all: one who'd been outside the bunker doors, the one she'd been about to shoot a few moments ago, plus the search party of four sent out to find James. She decided to take a chance. Whatever Dan had done further along the corridor had stopped troopers coming up behind her. These six troopers could be dodged – there were a lot of places to hide between here and the elevator. If she could avoid them, she might still be able to locate James.

She repeated the steps which had kept her concealed previously, deciding to take cover in the dorms where she'd left her laptop. She hesitated at the door, remembering that Nat had had to open it previously, this thing required clearance. She activated the sym node on her hand. It fired up straight away and she touched the entry pad. She heard a beep within the helmet, and the door slid open. Wearing the helmet must have authenticated the sym node in some way, and that meant she'd probably be able to access the elevators as well. She hoped so.

But something else was happening too. Since she'd placed the helmet on her head, she'd begun to hear the mutterings of somebody who sounded distressed, in pain even. All she could sense was a confused flow of thoughts, commands and plans. She didn't know it then, but she was receiving the streamed consciousness of the Queen. To her it was a jumbled mass of words and information – she was unable to filter it or process it in any way. In spite of that, Amy got a strong sense of who – or what – was conveying this data. It was female and she was in a high state of anguish and agitation. Whatever she was doing, she was doing unwillingly. Such was the force of the sadness that she picked up, Amy had to tear off the helmet, she couldn't bear it any longer.

She grabbed her laptop from the bed where hours before she'd first found the overalls which had served so well, letting her blend in. As she picked it up, she noticed something she'd missed before. There was an SD card tucked into the side, just the tip of it protruding. Amy didn't have an SD card, and her instinct made her wonder if that's what Nat had been up to when she'd found her in the car.

She'd check it later. She could hear the troopers moving along the corridor outside. They'd be in here soon. She grabbed one of the metal wardrobes – it was easy to shift, and she pulled it in front of herself in a corner. There was just enough room for her to conceal herself.

The troopers entered the room – two stood outside the doorway, four came inside. They threw whoever they'd been carrying onto one of the beds. They searched the room, under beds, in wardrobes and cupboards, but they didn't detect or hear Amy in her makeshift hiding place. They left the dorm, the door closed behind them and Amy began breathing easily again.

She intuitively knew who it was on the bed, but she had to see for herself. Amy rushed up to the body and turned it over gingerly. She felt for a pulse, in the neck and in the wrist. Blood and mud were caked in equal measure over his body and clothes. It was James. And he was dead.

Cleaning Up

As soon as Kate had been released from the power of the device in her neck, the Queen had come online and taken over control of the troopers. From that moment she was able to broadcast a steady stream of information and instructions directly to all troopers, whichever Quadrant they were in.

She could see and hear everything that they could. It was a constant stream of a thousand consciousnesses, a disjointed jumble to anybody but the Queen and the troopers who'd been modified to receive this data. The Queen had gained this position because she had powers beyond those of her warriors. She was telepathic, and it was her genetic ability that had been harnessed to create this terrible army, part human, part machine.

The Queen's power was exerted too late to stop the Unification process, which had been sanctioned by the Global Consortium, but it didn't matter to the perpetrators of these crimes. They had only needed the Nexus. Now they had a vast spaceship at their command, it would all be destroyed in the end anyway.

Thousands of miles below, in the three Quadrants that had been overcome by troopers, bunker personnel were being rounded up and contained on the remaining upper levels. Those who resisted were killed, the others herded callously into cramped rooms. There they would perish once the final bunker assault had been completed, but in the meantime they'd be held as hostages, useful currency to hasten the conclusion of this battle.

Troopers who'd been stationed in the lower levels of the Quadrants were now in space and docked with the Nexus. They could move freely between each of the Nexus Quadrants, but there were only two ways on and off this ship since the fifth button had been activated by Nat. Either it required docking from space, or there was one central Nexus transporter – everything that came on or went off this hub went through a single portal. Only the third Quadrant remained uncaptured on the ground. Once the Nexus was fully mobilized, the final assault would begin.

The Nexus had been conceived as an ark, a refuge for humanity to start all over again if the terraforming had failed. Now it represented the last remnants of a dead society. It would come crashing down onto the surface of the planet that had created it, destroyed by a human whose hatred for his species knew no limits. It was only a matter of time now. The shards had begun to change the Earth's biosphere, after a certain amount of time that process was unstoppable. The last tatters of the human race would be defenceless against it.

Very soon, this planet would take its last breath, the sleeping life forms on the surface below perishing in the process. But who would be left to hear Earth's final screams?

The Devil's Offer

As I came round I was aware of a sharp pain in my head. For a few moments I was disorientated, but then I pieced things together. I was on the floor in a control room similar to those I'd seen in the Quadrants. I looked around and saw Nat on the floor next to me. There was blood too, but it wasn't hers. I looked to the other side of me, and there, motionless and bruised on the floor, was Doctor Pierce.

I was battling through my sore head now, and Nat had begun to wake. She barely had her eyes open before she leaped up and ran with terrible force at somebody who was standing across the room. She hurled herself at him as if she didn't care about the outcome, scratching his face, drawing blood, before a trooper pulled her off and threw her back to the floor. I studied her target. It was Doctor Pierce. Well, it was somebody who looked like Doctor Pierce. A clone perhaps? A twin more likely. They were the same, yet not the same. Identical twins, but one had a kinder face – the man who was lying unconscious at my side. I recognized that tie of his. It was doing that weird thing again where it seemed to reflect different colours.

The man I was staring at had hate in his eyes, he looked wild and mad. There was somebody else beside him. At first I mistook him for a human, but he wasn't quite human. That was confirmed when I clocked his hands – he had loads of fingers, seven on each hand. Wow!

Nat was dazed. A trooper came up and restrained her with his booted foot. She looked as if she was only taking a few moments out before she got up for round two.

The mad-looking Doctor Pierce began to speak.

'Welcome, Dan ... and Nat. How nice it is to see you both together again.'

'You scumbag!' yelled Nat. She struggled against the trooper's restraint and he hit her with his weapon. Blood trickled from her forehead. She was subdued now, although from what I'd seen of Nat recently she was just waiting for her moment. As I went to protect her, another trooper moved towards me menacingly.

Pierce carried on speaking. Nat had taken quite a gash out of his face.

'Thank you for coming to me, it saved me a lot of time having to flush you both out. I must say, I thought we'd be retrieving your dead bodies. The fact that you're both alive is a very pleasant bonus.'

Okay, this was definitely not the Doctor Pierce I knew at school. Sure, that guy was weird and difficult to talk to, but his evil twin had an even bigger attitude problem. This guy was hardcore nasty. The Doctor Pierce who was lying at my side began to stir, roused to consciousness by the commotion.

'Dan ...' he said, looking at me, then '... and Nat too.'

The look on his face told me all I needed to know. This was not good.

'Henry!' he shouted at the other man. 'You need to stop this now!'

'Shut up, Harold!' came the reply, and a trooper raised his weapon as if about to strike the man at my side. He was cowed. They'd done this to him already, like Nat. He knew they'd use violence if we gave them the excuse.

'Dan, you already know my brother Harold Pierce. Nat – meet the other Doctor Pierce, my useless twin.'

So they were twins. At least we had something in common. I suppose it was a starting point, though I got the feeling we wouldn't be doing a lot of bonding.

'I'm sure you've already figured out, Nat, why you were my guest in the lab for so long. I see from your comms tabs that you've got nice little timers counting down to the end. Less than two hours remaining. I hope you're enjoying your final minutes of life.'

Okay, this guy was really starting to annoy me now. I could see why Nat disliked him so much. It seemed like they knew each other already.

'Of course, it was your sister who helped us engineer all of this. Without access to her DNA for the past three years, none of this would have been possible. So, thank you, Nat. You've done me a huge service – but for Earth, I'm afraid it's not so good.'

Nat struggled again. I could almost feel the hatred seeping from her, she couldn't wait to hurt this man.

'I want to give you the opportunity of life, though, my young friends,' he continued, clearly enjoying the power he wielded here. His weirdo friend, the fingers guy, was smiling, enjoying being a spectator in all of this.

'My dear brother over there knows the truth about you two. I take it he hasn't chosen to share it with you yet?'

I looked at the other Doctor Pierce. He appeared concerned – I sensed we were nearing the truth now.

'Did you know that you're not even human?'

We'd had a hint of this from Xiang, but this was getting interesting.

'You know you are adopted, but did anybody ever tell you about your mother?'

Nat and I were hanging on his every word. The Doctor Pierce at my side started to speak.

'You don't have to do this, Henry. Have some compassion, for goodness' sake—'

On a nod from Henry Pierce, a trooper struck his twin with his weapon and he collapsed on the floor beside me. I was shaken by the violence used to hit him. I'd never seen aggression like it – I was scared, but angry too.

'Your mother was from another planet, the lovely planet of Zatheon, which you won't know about, of course. The reason I'm so pleased you're alive is that it gives us a chance for a final deal, a little arrangement that will save your lives. I told my friend Zadra Nurmeen here that you'd never take up my offer, but he's the psychological expert and he disagrees. So here's my offer, Nat and Dan ...'

He was enjoying this. He paused for dramatic effect, as if he were about to reveal the winner of a TV talent contest.

'Your real mother is still alive. Her name is Davran Saloor and she'd dearly love to see you again. You were both torn away from her in the first place – she screamed for days when she was separated from you.'

He had our attention now. We looked at each other. Of course we wanted to hear more.

'Here's the deal,' he continued, his eyes narrowing now.

'You get to live and meet your real mother—'

'And we have to do what?' Nat spat at him.

'In return, you have to help me to kill her planet.'

CHAPTER EIGHT

Vengeance

Amy allowed herself a moment to grieve over James, but knew she didn't have the luxury of time. She held his hand and her eyes began to well up with tears. As she looked at his lifeless body she started to experience another emotion, one which quickly overwhelmed her – anger.

Her kids were at risk, her friend had been killed, and a bunch of madmen were trying to destroy everything. If there had been anything left of the victim in Amy, it was gone now. For many years she'd been tamed by her experiences in the army, frightened off by such a near miss, and had been happy to settle for a life of domestic simplicity. Of course she'd loved it – the kids, Mike and everything – but in her working life she'd compromised. She'd never really fitted in to the nine-to-five office routine.

Amy picked up her laptop and popped out the SD card she'd so nearly missed. She put it safely in her pocket, placed the trooper's helmet back on her head, picked up her weapon and the laptop, and steeled herself for what was going to happen next.

She was blasting her way out of this corridor and getting back to Quadrant 3. And as sure as anything she was taking down some troopers on the way.

Crime

The reason for Davran Saloor's sudden and abrupt fall from grace was totally predictable. Her contribution to the early terraforming plans for Earth had been considerable. Without her knowledge and experience, the work would never have got off the ground in the first place.

Which is why so many efforts were made on Earth – and on Zatheon – to try to plead her case, to save her from the strict consequences of breaking the agreed protocols within the Covenant. The rules were there for a reason – they had been agreed by all twelve planets within the Off World Federation. Earth and Zatheon were two lone voices among those clamouring for punishment.

Yet Davran's crime was not one of evil or malice, it was a crime as old as time itself. She had simply fallen in love while on Earth, with a human who was not directly connected with the Genesis 2 project. So much of Earth and Zatheon biology was similar. There were just a few crucial evolutionary steps which made the difference.

Davran looked completely human, so it was no wonder that when she accidentally bumped into one of the military personnel at the high security facility in the UK where the Genesis 2 project was based, a connection was established and a friendship followed on from it. Locked away at the camp, so far away from her home planet and her sister, spending many hours with the rude and arrogant Zadra, the two Doctor Pierces and the other Genesis 2 personnel, it was inevitable that she'd crave new company. And she was a scientist too. Regardless of the rules, she was keen to learn more about this planet which was so similar to her own, yet with a population so much more fragmented and violent.

As her friendship with the guard – Jeff – grew, they took greater and greater risks. In fact, many people knew what was going on and turned a blind eye to it, such was Davran's invaluable contribution to the project, but when it became clear that she was carrying a child, a rapid intervention took place. At the time it was suspected that it was Zadra Nurmeen who had tipped off the Off World Federation, but nothing could be proven, and shortly afterwards he too was banished from the project.

With Davran pregnant and the Off World Federation now party to that information, the legal process had to be seen to be applied. The elders on Zatheon shook their heads in despair. They knew and loved Davran. She was not only a highly respected mineralogist, but also a well-liked colleague and adviser. A friend. Yet they understood it could have been anybody on any one of the twelve planets who had made this simple error – it was hardly a crime, but it could not go unpunished.

Davran was not carrying a single child, she was carrying twins. All Zatheon females gave birth to twins, it was part of what made their species unique. An evolutionary step on their planet had determined that twins sharing certain genetic traits were stronger physically and mentally than infants born alone. Zatheon twins had a symbiotic relationship – they were deeply connected from the moment of conception. As they grew from infants to adults, that connection became stronger, ultimately resulting in the ability to communicate telepathically. Their knowledge and wisdom were shared and each sibling could give strength to the other, so in times of illness the healthy twin could assist in the regeneration of the other. In evolutionary terms it had made the Zatheons a stronger, wiser and more temperate people, and in turn, their progression and achievements had soared.

It was already known that Zatheons and humans were capable of successfully procreating. In fact, an incident during the late 1960s was one of the reasons why the interplanetary legislation had been tightened up in the first place. It was untenable that more advanced technology and learning should be permitted to permeate other planets, allowing them to accelerate their progress at greater than natural evolutionary rates.

Davran and Jeff knew the rules. They understood the risks and they were compelled to accept the punishment. But when retribution came, it would have devastating consequences for both of them.

Rage

I slowly got up from the floor, trying to work out if anything was broken. For a man who'd just offered us a deal, Henry Pierce wasn't much of a diplomat. Nat, Harold Pierce and I had been thrown into a meeting room and given fifteen minutes to think through the proposition. To save our lives, would Nat and I agree to help destroy another planet? He'd included his own brother in that offer too, in spite of having beaten him up pretty badly.

Doctor Pierce wasn't looking good – he was still out cold. Like me, Nat was shaken by such brutal treatment. We looked at each other. I knew what she was thinking. The funny thing was, I really did know what she was thinking. That connection we'd lost when we were parted, well it seemed to be getting stronger the more time we spent together. She was experiencing it as well.

We nodded in agreement before saying anything. Of course we weren't taking up this offer. We desperately wanted to meet our birth mother – Henry Pierce couldn't have dropped a bigger bombshell on us if he'd tried. The fact that we weren't strictly human made sense. I wasn't particularly shocked – I felt exactly the same as I'd always done, when I didn't know my mum was from another planet. I was who I'd always been, but it just happened to be part human, part alien.

I'd known something was different about me ever since Nat and I were torn apart by the accident. My trouble at school wasn't only a strong reaction to death, it was always something more than that. It wasn't just grief either, it meant something much bigger to me when Nat was in the accident – it was a physical reaction for me, not only an emotional one. Now we were together again, we could both feel the strength of the bond between us. I could actually feel her anger and hatred towards Henry Pierce. It was unnerving – I'd never experienced such powerful emotions myself. I sensed it would burn her up if she didn't control it, it was clouding her judgement. If Nat didn't get a grip on this, she could make a bad decision – and considering where we were right then, it might destroy us all.

Target

. . .

Viktor recognized Magnus for the man he was. Highly intelligent, innovative and a collaborator. A man he felt he could trust, one he could do business with.

Together they hatched a plan and the deal was done. With no world leaders to sanction their actions, they were the planet's protectors, its sole custodians. But Viktor always had a backup plan. Sure, he'd made this agreement with Magnus over the nukes, and they'd need Xiang to sanction it too, but in matters of conflict and war he'd always found it best to have a Plan B.

So while Magnus fixed in preliminary strategic coordinates for the jointly controlled nukes, Viktor was plotting out his own strategy for the fifty nuclear weapons under his sole command, lying in wait beneath the cold waters of the Black Sea. These nukes, if they were needed, would be going somewhere completely different.

At that moment Viktor would not have been able to contemplate that within the next two hours he would be setting in the coordinates to deliver this nuclear payload to a destination in his own country.

CHAPTER NINE

Exiled

Many Zatheon elders would have been happy for their people to integrate with humans, but if the rules were changed, less socially evolved planets such as Helyios 4 would have been able to play the same game.

Several elders felt that increased interaction with Earth would bring a new dimension to their planet, one of greater passion and emotion, elements which some felt were lacking in their ordered world. It was a widely held belief among the majority of the Off World Federation members that Helyios 4 was best left to develop at its own slow rate. The less impact from that particular planet the better, but their voice still had a right to be heard within O-Fed itself. So it was that Davran found herself banished to an *ISOCell* in space. This was a humane punishment – she was fed, clothed and permitted to live in relative comfort. But all communications with her own world – and Earth – were broken off. She was to remain in isolation indefinitely.

At the insistence of the Helyions she was not permitted to keep her babies. They were taken away from her as part of the punishment, to be resettled in a manner to be determined at a later date. This left an uneasy feeling among the Zatheon elders, but like the other members they were bound to the Covenant which had maintained peace among the twelve planets for many years now.

After much argument, and a delay of almost three years the children were moved from their high security nursery and settled with new parents on Earth. Davran had a twin on Zatheon and it was felt to be too much of a risk to let the children stay on that planet. There was a precedent here too – it had worked well before during the first incident in the sixties and it would surely be fine a second time.

So the twins were settled on Earth where their presence would go undetected. Doctor Harold Pierce took the lead on this, and quickly sourced a couple who were childless and seeking to adopt. They were delighted to be allocated twins. A boy and a girl. As the result of an accident five years earlier, their new mother had been unable to have children of her own, so she and her husband Mike were ecstatic to be offered orphan siblings, a ready-made family. They named them immediately – Dan and Nat – and they lived happily and undetected on Earth until the day on which it all began to unravel. The day when Henry Pierce violently entered their lives and took away the daughter – and sister – they had all loved so much.

Prospecting

Mike was spoiled for choice. The files opened one by one –

he didn't know where to start. He called over the team he'd been assigned to work with and talked them through how he'd managed to break through the encryption. If he hadn't felt under such pressure to find any scrap of information which could save Nat and Dan, he might have taken a moment to bask in the glory. After so long away from the workplace and looking after Dan at home it felt good to have the admiration of his colleagues once again. He checked his ego quickly, knowing there was no room for this now, the clock was ticking. Dan and Nat were relying on him and Xiang – they were their only two sources of hope in this terrible situation. Either Xiang would find a medical solution or he'd find the cause – or the cure – or at least some clue as to what was happening to them. A bit of basic data on the nature of the nanovirus would help everybody gain some ground.

He quickly allocated the files to his team members. They'd work through each of them swiftly and methodically, reporting anything that looked significant. But it was like looking for a needle in a haystack. The files seemed to hold every memo, note, observation or finding that had fed into the Genesis 2 project since the early 1990s. Mike tried to search on key terms, entering 'Dan', 'Nat', 'Troywood', and any other word or phrase that he could think of to try and collate the information. But the data was not indexed in a way that he could quickly grasp. It reminded him of the Dewey Decimal system they used in libraries. It probably made sense to somebody, but it certainly made no sense to him. There was only one thing for it, he'd have to go one file at a time. They were prospecting for gold, eventually one of them would find a nugget.

But would it be in time to save Dan and Nat?

. . .

Prisoners

Harold Pierce was stirring at our side. He was badly bloodied and bruises were starting to show where he'd been so violently beaten. At least we now knew why Doctor Pierce seemed to have been acting like two people. It was because there were two Doctor Pierces – twins, just like us. Well, not exactly like us – they were identical, which of course Nat and I couldn't be.

I had never particularly warmed to Harold, who must have been the twin who came to help me through my 'difficulties' at school. That made sense – he knew more about me than I did myself. I suppose he'd have been the first person to be called in when the alien kid started playing up in the classroom.

It was strange – I'd received life-changing news in the past half-hour, but it was just making me feel calmer. In many ways, it explained who I was. I felt more comfortable in my own skin. Before these events I'd wondered what was wrong with me.

Harold lifted his head and began to speak.

'Dan ... are you kids okay?'

He seemed to be getting his priorities a bit wrong – if he could see what we saw, he'd be thinking more about himself. He was in a right state.

'I'm so sorry it's come to this. I thought I could protect you from what's happening. I had no idea my brother was planning these events, I should have known ...'

His voice trailed off, he looked broken. Nat chimed in to fill the silence.

'That guy outside – and his sidekick – they're the ones who took me.'

She paused, thinking back to what had happened. I got a glimpse of it in my own mind, a terrible image of her pain and loneliness – it shocked me. For a moment I was overwhelmed as I began to comprehend what she'd been through.

'He must have been the guy I saw when you were hit by that car, Nat,' I picked up. 'I was sure I'd seen you move when they put you in the ambulance. He was there when it happened.'

It was beginning to make sense now, the disparate pieces were coming together. Henry Pierce must have engineered the accident to get his hands on Nat. Maybe he wanted both of us, and perhaps if I hadn't stepped back it might have been me who'd disappeared for three years. I felt a surge of gratitude towards Nat, like I owed her one for what she'd been through. It might just as easily have been me. It was a safe bet that the nanovirus which was about to destroy us both was engineered via the experiments that were carried out on Nat.

Doctor Pierce started to talk again. He was in pain and it was difficult for him to speak, but he was determined to get the words out.

'I need to tell you some things before they come in here to get us again. If my brother is involved, it's very unlikely that this will end well for me. You know that you're twins and that your mother was not from this planet. Her name was Davran and she was a wonderful and intelligent woman. It broke her heart when she lost you children. I promised her I would take care of you both.'

He was getting quite emotional talking about this woman who was our mother and I sensed a lot of water had gone under the bridge to get everybody to where they were now. He talked about Amy – our mum – the only mum we'd ever known. He explained that we were symbiotic, which accounted for the connection I felt with Nat. As we got older, he said we'd become even more closely connected and develop a telepathy between us. He was a bit late with that one, it was happening already. This symbiosis was how Henry Pierce managed to infect Nat with the virus and spread it to me. It was like a virus passing wirelessly from one computer to another. When Nat and I met up again the reconnection took place and the destructive genetic process began. To be active it needed both of us together – alone it was completely benign.

Harold's guess was that his brother wanted us to act as carriers to destroy Zatheon – a Trojan horse to get the nanovirus that was destroying us embedded into the Zatheon population. We were his guinea pigs.

It was all a lot to take on board. Our comms tabs had been taken away from us, so I wasn't sure how much time we had left, but I knew it couldn't be long now. Simon and Kate were still at large on the ship. They must be up to something, so we had to trust we'd got people watching our backs. Our best strategy was to stall to buy more time. About ninety minutes at the maximum, by my reckoning. It was game over for me and Nat then, but if we could cheat our way through this, Henry Pierce might reverse the progression of the virus and Nat and I would get out of this alive. Harold agreed, but doubted there was any subterfuge he could use that would convince his brother. And then he dropped another bombshell on us. As if we hadn't had enough for one day.

'I need to tell you children that my brother and I are the same as you.'

Okay, we knew that. We could see they were twins. Nat was thinking the same as me – this telepathy thing was pretty cool. Harold could see that we didn't get it, so he carried on.

'You and Nat are luckier than Henry and me. We were the first twins born to a Zatheon mother and a human father.'

Okay, he had our complete attention now.

'It's why my brother and I were brought into the Genesis 2 project. Our capacity for learning and analysis is far superior to that of the average human, so we were obvious choices in many ways. But times were different when we were younger in the 1960s and they tried to suppress our non-human elements with drugs and experimental treatments. I attribute my brother's aggression to the treatments we were given – he's a brilliant scientist but also a troubled and dangerous man. I was lucky. I appear to have escaped from it with my sanity intact.'

Nat and I were silent. This was an amazing story.

'We've been separated for many years now,' he continued. 'Our symbiotic connection was severed a long time ago. Not unlike what you will be experiencing now, our connection will grow only stronger now we're reunited. As is the Zatheon way, we will battle it out in our heads, my consciousness fighting with his to come to a mutual resolve. He will know soon enough that we're trying to stall him, and he will quickly tire of my voice in his head urging restraint and compassion. When we were young he would torture me by pouring scalding hot water over me.' Again he paused. This was difficult for him. 'Now I have no doubt. When he's tired of me again, he will kill me. And it will be spiteful when he does it.'

Stealth

. . .

Simon and Kate knew they'd have troopers on their tail before long, so they weaved as erratic a course as they could through the ship. Simon, in particular, was able to make sense of how this vast structure in the heavens fitted together. The corridors on Levels 3 and 4 of each Quadrant had been curved, while the upper levels were straight and regular. It was like a giant pizza in space, each Quadrant forming one slice – or quarter – of the structure.

It was all based on a careful plan: they'd built in weaponry areas; they could fully re-populate here using the embryos that Dan and Nat had found earlier; they had a fighting force – the very troopers they were running to avoid – and they had the ability to grow their own food up here. It was all very clever, and Simon began to recognize how in many ways he'd helped to create this. He reflected on all the people he'd transported over the years – the scientists, the politicians, the ordinary members of the public. He'd carried out countless surveillance missions, many seemingly random tasks, but he saw now how all of that work had come together. He felt a sense of relief that the work he'd done was not all bad. Sure, something had happened that day with Nat, but it was looking more and more like it had been the result of interference from elsewhere. Perhaps it was an early glimpse of the sabotage that was to come.

Whatever it was, the answers were beginning to flow now, and most importantly – amazingly – Nat was alive still. He and Kate would need to find the heart of this place, that's where the battle would need to be taken. He wasn't sure what the plan was yet, but he knew they needed to see their enemy, they had to know who – or what – they were up against. He'd agreed with Kate that once they'd shaken off the troopers, they'd start moving back towards the centre. It made sense that the main operation would be run from there.

The corridors were still unusually quiet. It seemed they had no plans to use these Quadrants – the troopers must have been making for some other place. They'd just passed back from the outer rim of the ship – what had previously formed the lower two floors of the bunkers – into the central Orb, the part of this craft in which was sited the main technical hub.

Simon had just ducked into a side room with Kate to avoid a passing trooper patrol. They took a moment to look around. They were in a vast hangar – it appeared to be disused, there were dust sheets over some of the equipment racks. Simon pulled off a few of the covers to look a little closer. As more and more equipment was revealed, they both began to realize what this was. They looked at each other. They'd been here before. This was where they'd been immersed in the simulation exercise all those years ago. The experiments had not taken place on Earth, as they'd thought, they'd been carried out up here, in space. No wonder they were transported under sedation, it would be imperative to keep this location completely confidential.

And what of the strange figure they'd both seen in the corner just before they were rendered unconscious? It had seemed like a ridiculous fantasy at the time, a preposterous explanation. They'd barely dared to even venture the idea to each other. But now they were certain. They were dealing with off-planet matters here and whatever was waiting for them on this ship, it was not of their world.

CHAPTER TEN

The Precedent

The children were sitting up in their high chairs, playing happily and laughing at each other. The doctor felt a pang of guilt about what he was about to do.

The birth of these children had rocked the Off World Federation to its core. It was still early days for Earth within O-Fed and as the lead scientist he'd had to stretch the boundaries of his belief and understanding to get to grips with the implications of it all. These children were the living consequence of what happened when different humanoid species began to procreate. At the time nobody had any idea what the outcome would be, neither humans nor Zatheons knew if the children would even be born alive.

The birth took place on Earth. The Zatheon mother was monitored securely from a military base in the United States. There was secret joy and wonderment when the twins turned out to be living and healthy. The Zatheon genes were dominant but in every respect these babies looked as if they had been born to human parents.

The positivity of seeing two new lives created in such a way turned swiftly to politics as pressure grew from other O-Fed members to manage the situation in line with agreed Covenant protocols. Certainly the Zatheon elders would have loved their people to mix with the humans, and even though opinions on Earth were much more guarded, there was a general consensus among O-Fed members – who numbered much fewer in the sixties – that this was not such a terrible thing to happen. But as new members of the Off World Federation, Earth's representatives were unsure of their position, terrified of provoking an attack from planets more sophisticated than their own, and preferring not to make waves. This would change as Earth technology accelerated in leaps and bounds, and humanity in turn became much more of a threat to the other eleven planets within the interplanetary pact. But at that time this was a new and potentially threatening situation.

So it was decided, as it would be once again many years later, that the parents of these hybrid children would be punished for their transgression. They'd simply fallen in love, of course, but that was against O-Fed rules and – under duress from the Helyions – it was agreed that both parents would be ostracized. This meant being separated from each other, their planet and their people, and living in isolation in self-sustaining pods in space. *ISO*Cells. Their basic needs would be met, but they would be forever segregated from all other life.

This rankled with the Zatheons, who were a cerebral and merciful species, but it was driven through by the Helyions. Even in the sixties, before the plight of both Earth and Helyios 4 was fully understood, the Helyions seemed to have earmarked Earth. They took a special interest in the planet and were extremely keen that its technology did not accelerate any faster than it would via natural evolution. They were particularly eager to separate Zatheons and humans, as if they could sense the natural affinity between the two worlds and were determined to stop the relationship dead in its tracks. Their reasons would become clear almost half a century later.

This left the doctor with an ethical dilemma. His Hippocratic oath was to do no harm, but would what he was about to do help these children or hurt them? He consoled himself with the thought that animal testing had brought massive advances to man. Indeed, it was animal testing that had first brought Earth to the attention of the Off World Federation. The dog Laika and Albert II, the Rhesus monkey, had both been calculated risks at the time, but the experiments had resulted in successful space tests, paving the way for future human breakthroughs.

So, as he prepared the drug trials for the twins, he fought against his instinct to do only good by reconciling the doubts in his mind. This was an important scientific study, a huge opportunity to observe the first ever human–Zatheon hybrids. The Off World Federation would learn much from this, and in future years it might pave the way for closer ties between one another, perhaps even multi-species life on different planets. As the first travellers on Earth had explored and spread across the globe so many hundreds of years ago, when the first ocean-going boats had been built, perhaps the same would now happen in space. And it all would have started with him, in this medical facility, with these twins.

The choice was made on a whim. Harold was to receive the placebo, Henry was to be given the experimental drug treatment. It could so easily have been the other way around. The fates of two individuals were decided on that day, and no single person would ever be held accountable for the damage inflicted upon Henry Pierce as a result of those trials. But the harm done to him would be irreparable and fifty years later the whole world would be held to account for its silent acquiescence.

Cloaked

The darkness surrounding the planet had taken on a blue hue now. It was still haunting, impenetrable and all consuming, but Terra Level 2 was reaching its conclusion. This was the crucial next stage of the terraforming of Earth. The preparatory work was completed and what followed next would determine the planet's future.

Undetected by the satellite monitoring sentinels surrounding Earth, an event had taken place that very few would ever know about. It would form the basis of a future alliance between Zatheon and Earth that would be kept from the Off World Federation for hundreds of years.

Unknown to even Henry Pierce, a cloaked ship from Helyios 4 had penetrated the satellite matrix surrounding the planet and entered the Earth's atmosphere. The Helyions were not supposed to be capable of creating such technology, yet here it was – they had deftly handled extended interplanetary travel, and nobody even knew about it. On any planet. They kept many secrets below the surface of Helyios 4, but this was the one best hidden, it was the core deception that they'd planned for many years now.

As the awkward, brutal-looking ship entered the Earth's

atmosphere, it made straight for a specific destination. Unseen by any monitoring or surveillance system, the Helyion ship hovered above Lake Karachay in western Russia, then began to sink slowly below the waters, like a hungry creature lying in wait.

This was the most radioactive place on the planet, the perfect location from which to create the first Helyion settlement on Earth.

Unbearable

Amy checked her weapon and made sure it was set to kill. She'd vowed all those years ago never to have anything to do with firearms again. And now the man who was responsible for her making that decision was dead.

In wounding James – and ultimately saving his life – she'd wielded a power she'd never wished to possess again. Yet here she was, almost twenty years later, with a weapon in her hand, less than a metre away from the body of the man whose injuries had forced that decision upon her as a 19 year old. She was angry – really angry – that she'd lost her friend. Sitting by his body, preparing to make her final escape from this wretched bunker, she knew she wasn't a killer and never had been. She didn't wish to become one either.

These troopers – however threatening they appeared, whatever damage they'd done – they were no more in control of their actions than she and James had been when the pulsating lights had been active in their own necks. They aren't responsible, she thought to herself. Whoever is orchestrating these events, they're the ones who should be accountable for this. She flicked the switch back to its stun setting. It was the right decision. She didn't want any deaths on her hands that day, she refused to pass judgement on who should live and who should die.

She was still wearing the trooper's helmet. Once again the female voice was coming through with a disturbing intensity. She couldn't make out the words, but she got an overwhelming sense of sadness and isolation. Whatever or whoever was controlling these troopers, this seemed to be the voice of a hostage trapped in a cycle of events that she was unable to escape. Amy pulled off the helmet. It was unbearable to listen to. She was about to discard it, when she thought better of it. She should take it back to Mike and Magnus – they might be able to make something of it. Perhaps they could work out what this voice was saying and where it was coming from.

She'd need to find a bag. She had a laptop and helmet to carry, as well as having to shoot her way out of trouble. There were a couple of rucksacks in the dorm. She'd been lucky to pass through the room twice now and to find what she needed to survive on both occasions. Amy slung one of the bags over her shoulders so that it was secure and out of her way, and paused by the door. The sym node was activated. The only thing that could scupper this escape plan was if the glove didn't work. Only one way to find out. She exited the dormitory. Damn, all six troopers were in the corridor, still looking for her. Well, here she was.

Dan had prevented any more troopers entering the area by causing the explosion further along the corridor, but who knew how long that line of defence would hold? She had a momentary advantage. She aimed her weapon and shot wildly at the troopers. One down, two, three ... The remaining troopers were fast. One of them was running directly at her with a velocity which shook her for a moment. She fired again, hitting the trooper, but not managing to stop him. She braced herself for the impact as he struck her with massive force, bringing her to the ground.

She felt a sharp pain from the wounds that had so recently healed. She flinched, but there was no time to recover. The trooper who'd floored her had struck her with such force that he'd damaged his helmet visor as he crashed into the floor. He'd have to remove the helmet to continue his assault. The remaining two troopers had weapons drawn, but were waiting to see what damage their colleague had done. It seemed they had instructions to apprehend, not kill her. For a few seconds Amy lay still, to sow the seed of doubt in their minds and buy a small time advantage. As the trooper to her side started to get to his feet, she turned over fast, shooting the two remaining troopers ahead of her and bringing them down.

She got up to run along the corridor towards the elevator, but the now helmetless trooper grabbed her ankle. She pounded his hand with the end of her weapon. His instinctive reaction was to let go of her foot to avoid the blow. He might have been part-machine, but there was still a human in there with human reactions. She ran for her life, leaping over the unconscious bodies of the other troopers. She was aware of the man behind her preparing to run at her again. He was fast. Very fast. He was gaining on her. Damn this long corridor, it seemed to go on forever.

As she saw the elevator entrance ahead of her, she looked down to check the sym node on her hand. To the other side of the elevator she could hear the sound of running feet. It was the other troopers. They had broken through the debris from the explosion. Amy drew her weapon, slammed against the elevator entrance and pressed the button to open the doors.

Suddenly the trooper on her tail caught up with her, slamming into her with such force it took her breath away. Part of her wanted to crumple to the floor, to give up the fight, but she was determined to get through this. She had to get the helmet and the SD card to Quadrant 3 and she was going to do everything she could to save Dan and Nat.

The trooper was about to strike her head. His speed was inhuman, he seemed to be supercharged, Amy could barely keep up with him. She took another blow, she could feel herself slipping out of consciousness, but with one huge and final effort she leaped into the elevator as the doors opened. The trooper hesitated for a moment, as if he'd doubted himself momentarily, then he followed her into the elevator, ready to resume the blows to her body. As he picked Amy up by her hair, she struck out and hit the buttons to her side. The doors slid shut just as the other troopers drew up outside.

The transporter lights activated and Amy sank to the ground, finally beaten by the ferocity of the trooper's blows.

CHAPTER ELEVEN

The First Trooper

Davran Saloor didn't know what had happened to the father of her children. The last she saw of him was at the end of their trial. There was never any question about their guilt, only the nature of the punishment that would be applied.

The proceedings were held within the confines of an O-Fed court hearing, with one representative from each planet presiding over their fate. The Helyions had intimidated the nine remaining parties – with the exception of Earth and Zatheon – into voting with them. The representatives from Earth and Zatheon felt as if they were presiding over a terrible injustice, but were powerless to intervene. Davran Saloor was ostracized with immediate effect.

Scattered throughout their respective universes were pods – ironically, created with Zatheon technology – in which criminals were placed in isolation. This had been agreed in the early days, when there had only been three members of the Off World Federation. There was no reprieve, this is where you spent the remainder of your days. For Zatheons, that was a very long time. Their lifespan was twice that of human beings. The oldest Zatheon had been known to live for 207 Earth years in almost perfect health.

Davran was immediately shipped away to an ISOCell, destined never to see the father of her children – or the twins – ever again. She was sentenced first, and she never knew what had happened to Jeff. According to the rules of the Covenant, he should have spent the rest of his life ostracized as well, the same fate that had been deemed suitable for Davran. But there was further Helyion interference here, an unprecedented departure from the Covenant and an agreement made between certain allies – and those too scared to resist. At the O-Fed meeting, as far as the Zatheons were concerned, Jeff had been ostracized. He would be allocated a random ISOCell and no one would ever know where he'd been abandoned in space. It could be anywhere in the eight known universes.

But as he was being escorted for transportation, there was some sleight of hand. O-Fed documentation certainly showed that he'd been ostracized, but the truth was a different story. Jeff had been procured for research purposes. This was instigated by a Helyion known as Zadra Nurmeen, who would himself be alienated along with his friend Henry Pierce in the years that followed.

They'd be removed from the Genesis 2 project on moral and ethical grounds. That could mean a number of things. In their case it related to crimes against humanity. To be specific, experimentation on live human beings, using exoskeleton technology procured from an innovative young entrepreneur whose company was known as Magnum Enterprises.

. . .

Control

Henry Pierce felt that he'd been born for this moment. His useless brother was incarcerated and soon he'd be dead or shackled in a laboratory somewhere, helping Henry to achieve supremacy among the remaining O-Fed planets. Either way, he'd kill Harold eventually. And now he was surrounded by the faces of the world's leaders. They'd been forced to watch the scenes that had just been played out on the main deck of the Nexus. Paralysed by the darkness on Earth, only able to communicate via subconsciousness and holographic representations, they were powerless to do anything.

They could debate and vote all they wanted to. There was only one vote that counted now, and that was his own. How good it felt to be able to force these treacherous wretches to watch as he destroyed their planet. Many of the faces on these screens had been behind his ejection from the Genesis 2 project all those years earlier. These members of the Global Consortium had turned their backs on him and now they'd pay for it.

They protested at him via their screens, but as the voices grew too loud, he simply muted them. The power was all his and it felt good. But there was one voice left. He didn't hear it at first, and one by one he silenced the protestations of the world's leaders, helplessly pleading with him and offering to make deals to save the planet. This was a familiar voice. It was the voice of his brother, creeping back into his head after all those years apart. At one time, as they'd worked on the Genesis 2 project together, it had been a constant, a welcome source of information, theory and learning which had hastened their progress. It had even been companionable and he'd felt calmer as a result. However, the voice was long since lost after Henry had been so forcibly ejected from Genesis 2. Now it was back, but soon his brother's voice would be silenced for good. Either Harold would agree to work with him on the destruction of Zatheon or he'd be ejected into space via the airlocks.

In fact, whatever happened, his brother was eventually leaving via the airlocks ... it was simply a matter of the timing.

Manipulation

Mike was horrified and intrigued at what he'd just read in the document. He tried to stop himself getting immersed in the details, there was so much information within those files. He had to focus on the priorities, finding information to help Dan and Nat. This file blew his mind – he'd grown up with conspiracy theories and rumours of Area 51, but this was the real thing. It dated back to 1967, to the birth of twins. To an alien mother. Like Dan and Nat perhaps. But it was the name that captured his attention most.

He nearly missed it at first, because initially they'd just used the alien names of the children. Ajnur 1 and Ajnur 2. That had changed over time – the doctor in charge of the twins had obviously grown attached to them. After a while they were referred to as Henry and Harold.

Then some kind of experimental trial had begun and the references had changed again. But it seemed that whoever had handwritten those original notes in the sixties, before they were scanned into the records, had needed to disassociate himself from whatever was happening to one of the children. Henry Pierce was simply referred to as 'Child 002' until the adoption was completed. But it was quite clear that his behaviour had deteriorated rapidly after the drug trials began. You could almost sense the relief from whoever was caring for these children when the final adoption update on the twins was entered into the official records.

Adoption date: 3rd May 1969

Parents: Andrew and Jean Pierce

Observations: Child 002 behaviour suppressed c/o maximum dosage of Tantrazinol/078-Y, prior behaviours violent and erratic. Parents delighted to adopt twins, desperate to start family.

Recommendations: No further trials, severe adverse effects. Destroy adoption paperwork, recommend no trackbacks at O-Fed level.

File closed: 5th May 1969

Revelations

Harold Pierce was exhausted. He may have been bruised and weary, but he was determined to share as much as he could with us.

'Who is our real mum?' asked Nat. We were both

desperate to learn more about her. I couldn't even remember her name.

'I never knew what happened to her,' Doctor Pierce began. 'There was a lot of trouble with O-Fed at that time.'

We looked at him, and Nat had to spell it out.

'Off World Federation?'

'Yes, that's right. Remember, I told you in my video feed that the darkness is connected to the terraforming of Earth, Dan?' I nodded and he carried on talking. 'Well, it's not Earth technology that we're using. Very little of what you've seen in the bunkers is human technology.'

I knew it! There was no way you could buy this stuff from your local PC store – if you could, the Tracy family would have spotted it long ago. And bought all of it.

'The Off World Federation is made up of twelve planets, Earth being one of them. The terraforming has to take place now, or there won't be a world capable of sustaining human life when you two grow up. It's my guess that Henry is planning to sabotage it. If Zadra Nurmeen is here, they're looking after the interests of Helyios 4, they certainly won't be concerned about Earth.'

This was too much to take in, all this talk of planets and weird names that meant nothing to me. Nat was more on the ball.

'I know that strange guy already. I saw him on the PC screen in the lab – I only got a glimpse, but it was definitely him.'

Doctor Pierce looked full of shame, and he began to apologize to Nat.

'Nat, I'm so sorry I didn't see what happened to you afterwards. I thought it was a genuine accident – I was sure you were dead ...'

He was choked and having difficulty talking about this.

He seemed to know what Nat had been put through over the past three years.

'I honestly didn't know you were alive until I saw you on the screens ... until your mum went to see you in the car park outside the bunker, and even then I couldn't be sure it was you. It came together for me then – it began to make sense to me when we had the delays with the lighting. It had to be my brother. He was the only one capable of sabotaging this project. He played it well, though. Goodness knows how he kept it hidden all these years. I would never have known they were planning this.'

As if on cue, three troopers burst into the room. They escorted us roughly back to the ops area where Henry Pierce was addressing the worried faces on the screens surrounding him. I scarcely recognized any of them. Only two looked familiar. I was sure one of them was the president of the United States, and the other was our prime minister. Neither seemed real, they were like digital animations of some kind.

Henry Pierce's chum – Zadra Nurmeen or whatever he was called – just sat there, smiling to himself. He had a horrible, self-satisfied look on his face. He didn't say or do anything, he was watching Pierce's every move. Henry was gesticulating wildly as he goaded the people on the screens. As we were thrown to the ground a couple of metres away from him, he cut himself short.

'Ah, decision time!' he announced, clapping his hands together as if this were some family quiz show.

'We'll do it,' I said straight away. 'We'll help you.'

Nat thought that came a bit too easy, so she chipped in a 'Like hell we will!' for good measure. Pierce didn't know which of us to listen to and immediately became impatient. Talk about a sudden change of character. He walked over to

Harold and struck him across the face. No warning, no provocation, he just seemed to feel like doing it. I flinched, but Nat seemed to be familiar with this erratic behaviour.

'Take him to the airlock,' he shouted at one of the troopers. 'See if that'll help my brother make his mind up.'

As the trooper grabbed Harold by the shoulder and manhandled him out of the ops area, I could see that look on Nat's face again. I was beginning to be able to speak to her directly now – we were both getting better at it. I tried to use telepathy to tell her to calm down, to wait things out, but she wasn't having any of it. She couldn't help herself, she hated this man. She waited for him to pass close to her, and she leaped up and started to beat his face with her fists. Crazy he might have been, but he wasn't physically strong, so he had to take this beating for the few moments that it took the troopers to realize what was going on and to react to it.

Their response was violent and ruthless. They pulled Nat off Henry Pierce and threw her across the room, hitting her head against one of the consoles. I thought she was going to move, but then she passed out, unconscious. Blood trickled down her forehead.

Pierce went over to her, wiped some of the blood onto his finger and then walked up to me threateningly.

'You want more of this on your hands?' he hissed. He was furious at his humiliation in front of the faces on the screens.

'No,' I answered sheepishly. I didn't want to provoke him. I was furious with Nat – we couldn't afford all these temper tantrums and distractions, they were wasting time.

Pierce wiped away the blood on his face with the hand he'd been waving at me threateningly.

'I've had enough of this,' he suddenly declared. 'Make

up your mind – you're either with me or you take a trip into space with them.'

And to illustrate what he meant, he dished out his punishment to Nat.

'Take her to the airlock!' he screamed.

CHAPTER TWELVE

Defence

It was on 23 March 1983 – eight months before the formal Global Consortium agreement was made in November of that year – that President Ronald Reagan proposed the Strategic Defence Initiative. The aim was to develop the technology to intercept enemy nuclear missiles.

At the time it had seemed wildly ambitious in its scale, the stuff of science fiction, but it was only a cover for the work that would need to be done for the Genesis 2 project. Although the Star Wars initiative – as it was known – changed its name over the years, the integrity of the project remained intact, and it became fully integrated into the mission to save Earth from its rapidly approaching fate.

As cold war relationships evolved, mainly due to global governmental focus on the impending environmental catastrophe, the SDI became less about defence and more about creating a delivery system for the shards. It was these terraforming shards which would eventually be released via the satellite matrix surrounding the planet, using off-planet technology and processes which had been inspired by the early work of Davran Saloor. However, their defensive capability remained intact.

President Reagan's Strategic Defence Initiative had become a reality many years ago. Renamed by President Clinton ten years later as BMDO – or Ballistic Missile Defence Organization – it had in fact evolved way beyond its original scope. Unknown to the world's press – and largely a secret within Global Consortium circles – nuclear weaponry was, for all intents and purposes, a redundant technology. Ironically, the devices which we had built to destroy each other had become the vehicle of our salvation.

Now called the Global Defence Matrix, it was capable of detecting the signature of any nuclear missile anywhere in the world. The next generation of warfare would involve nanotechnology and genetic combat, but that was for a future which did not yet exist. The system of defence which had been built to protect us from each other would still have its part to play. When President Reagan announced the initiative decades ago, he could barely have imagined that it would eventually be used in the final battle for Earth.

Lake Karachay

The Helyion ship lay fully immersed below the waters of Lake Karachay, waiting patiently for the final terraforming process to begin. This had been planned long ago by the government on Helyios 4. The unique access to Earth afforded to their emissary Zadra Nurmeen and his strategic partnership with the Earth scientist Doctor Henry Pierce had been most advantageous to them. With only fifty-three Helyion years – or thirty Earth years – to go until the destruction of their planet, they couldn't take the risk of Earth's terraforming project not working.

It was experimental, even for the Zatheons, and in spite of the early assurances of Davran Saloor – and her successor after she was removed from the project – the Helyions were not going to leave anything to chance. Already Henry Pierce and Zadra Nurmeen had a plan in motion to sabotage the terraforming process and deliver the Earth to the Helyions as a dead, but still mineral rich, planet.

That was good, but unknown to Henry Pierce they'd also hatched a plan of their own. Call it a backup plan, in case Pierce was unable to deliver. Under cover of the terraforming darkness, they would land a craft in the most hospitable area they could locate on the planet. With the entire planet asleep, defence systems down, and nobody to monitor what they were doing, they would be able to slip through the matrix using the cloaking mechanism which nobody in the Global Consortium believed them to be capable of building. They'd all despised the Helyions, with their dark, industrial practices and rough physicality, but appearances had deceived, and they were capable of advanced scientific developments.

The Helyion ship would lurk within the contaminated waters of Lake Karachay while the terraforming process worked through to completion of Terra Level 3 on the surface above them. While it did so they would begin a detailed analysis of their own. They would sample the planet's mineral deposits and confirm the options for sustainability for their own species. If the Earth scientist and Zadra Nurmeen were successful, they would sabotage the terraforming and deliver a dead planet, one which they would have full rights under the O-Fed Covenant to plunder.

And if Pierce and Zadra Nurmeen failed? Well, they'd just take the planet anyway, thus causing the first interplanetary war since the Off World Federation had come into existence.

The Captive

Amy was not fully aware of what happened next, but when she thought back to it, she had noticed the moment at which the trooper had paused – only for a few seconds. Later she would understand that this was because the data stream from his helmet had been broken and he'd been disorientated, but it was this that eventually saved her life.

As the transporter lights activated, she lost consciousness, finally giving in to the power of the blows she'd received from him. She was half aware of what was going on around her as the transporter rematerialized on Quadrant 3. The doors to the elevator opened. As she drifted in and out of awareness, she clocked the explosives that had been packed around this area in case of attack. The minute the doors opened, several laser beams immediately lit up the area, all targeted on the trooper.

She didn't know it at the time, but they were both seconds away from being blown up. If the explosives expert that Magnus had put in charge down there had had less presence of mind, he'd have detonated them the minute they saw the trooper. As it was, it was the fact that he was not wearing a helmet that had caused hesitation. With no helmet on, the trooper became humanized. It was, after all, a human being in there, underneath the robotics and technological enhancements.

So Amy did not lose her life that day. The trooper was stunned and not killed, and the transporter remained intact, in readiness for use as the portal which would be used for the final invasion of Quadrant 3. She was vaguely aware of being taken on a hover trolley to the med lab, but she was unable to speak coherently, the force of the trooper's blows had taken their toll. And so it was that the items in her bag lay undiscovered. Items which could provide two essential pieces of information capable of dramatically changing the course of events.

Airlock

Henry Pierce was violent and completely unpredictable. One minute he appeared charming, the next he was exploding into uncontrolled rage.

I'd barely noticed it before, amid all the activity and threats, but there were other people here, besides the troopers. They were diminutive and were keeping their heads down, trying not to bait Pierce in any way. They appeared to be of Asian ethnic origin and looked scared out of their wits, like school children trying to avoid being noticed by the school bully.

One caught my attention in particular. He'd been trying to catch my eye without being noticed. I winced as I saw a scar across his face – barely healed, red and puffy. It looked as if it might be septic. It had been left untreated, that was for sure. This man didn't look as if he was here of his own free will.

The alien guy was quieter than Pierce, who seemed to have a need to make his presence felt. He just sat there taking it all in. He seemed to be the one in control here, his composure and self-assurance sinister and threatening.

From what I could pick up, they were getting ready to mount their final assault on Magnus's bunker now that the Quadrants were all locked in. Pierce signalled to one of the troopers to take me away. As he did so, the man who'd been trying to attract my attention pretended to drop a pen, immediately stooping to pick it up. His timing was excellent. He put an object in my hand as I was dragged through the ops area by the trooper. I barely paused as he handed it to me, you'd have to have been looking very carefully to see what had happened. But had Pierce seen what was going on? My heart thudded in my chest as he leaped up and strode across the room straight at the man. He pushed him to the floor, picked up the pen and chucked it at him, shouting at him not to be so careless. He hadn't spotted our interaction, after all.

I was thrown unceremoniously into the airlock with Nat and Harold Pierce. Pierce was out cold on the floor, while Nat sat dazed in the corner. The area had huge windows looking directly out into space. From here it was easier to get a sense of how the place was laid out. We were in a central, circular area and I could see how the four Quadrants had joined together to create an outer ring. Of course, this room opened directly into space: it was an airlock with little between us and oblivion. I tried not to dwell on how vulnerable that made us right then, especially with that madman just along the corridor in the ops area. Two troopers stood guarding the door to the outside. I'm not sure where they thought we might be going.

I turned to face Nat, as if I was going to speak to her,

but I was really concealing my actions from the surveillance camera behind me. Whoever that man was who risked Doctor Pierce's ferocious temper to pass these two things to me, he was obviously a friend. He'd handed me my comms tab for starters, and that meant we could at least alert Simon and Kate, maybe even Magnus. And there was a crumpled piece of paper with it too. I unfolded it and looked at what was written there. Just a name. It meant nothing to me. It read 'Dae-Ho'.

Blood Clue

Xiang was making good progress in her makeshift laboratory. She was thanking her lucky stars that she was surrounded by techies rather than biologists. She'd posted Dan and Nat's vital signs on a large screen in the work area – everybody here needed to be mindful of the pressure they were under.

The nano-trackers she'd placed in their bloodstreams sent a steady stream of data to her console. Nat appeared to be at 83 percent through the viral contamination process, Dan was still some way behind at 71 percent. But Xiang had noticed some interesting things happening on the screens, though she wasn't quite clear yet of their significance. Dan and Nat's adrenalin levels had soared, and as they did so it seemed to speed up the genetic degeneration that was taking place. That was only to be expected really, adrenalin flow tended to make all the body's functions run on overdrive.

She wondered what the twins were up to, but knew she mustn't get distracted, she had to focus on just one thing:

finding a solution to Dan and Nat's impending deaths. But there was something she couldn't explain. She reckoned the twins had about fifty-five minutes left, maybe less if she'd got her projections wrong. But both Nat and Dan's viral levels had suddenly gone down. Nat's had dropped to 69 percent, Dan's to 51 percent – in an instant they'd bought themselves another thirty to sixty minutes of life. What had just happened there?

Xiang tried to contact the twins via their comms tabs, but worryingly there was no reply. She immediately alerted Magnus, then returned to her analysis work. Focus, Xiang. You know the twins are alive, you can see the data on the screen, she reminded herself. Let Magnus deal with the immediate problem, it's my job to solve this one.

She stared hard at the information streams, trying to fathom the reason for this change. Then, from nowhere, a third stream of data came online. But how? The same genetic breakdown was occurring in a third person – but who was it? To be showing these signs, they would have to be the same genetic make-up as Dan and Nat – human hybrids. Xiang broke into a sweat as she realized the implications of this. There was another like Dan and Nat – and whoever it was had had this nanovirus transferred to them. It was transmissible to those with the correct biology. Human hybrids. It meant they were sharing the nanovirus between the three of them. The third person was showing low infection signs at only 5 percent through the genetic degeneration process. In fact, the figures for this third person were static, remaining at 5 percent, but it had been good for Dan and Nat, effectively it had bought them a little more time.

Xiang was working blind, she didn't know who the third person was or what had happened to cause this change. But she could extrapolate three pieces of key information from the data. Firstly, this nanovirus could be transferred from one host to another, and in so doing, it might prolong the life of somebody who was already infected. But what was the means of transfer – or transmission? Secondly, the genetic disintegration process was not one way; it could be reversed, speeded up or slowed down. That gave Dan and Nat a better chance – but it had only bought them minutes, not hours or days as she would have preferred.

Finally, and most importantly to Xiang, this data suggested that Dan and Nat were not unique, there was at least one other like them. That meant that she'd have a third subject for a possible transfusion, the process that Magnus's tech team were working on at that very moment. The nanovirus was man-made, although the carrier was biologically based, but that suggested the solution might be man-made too.

Nanotechnology could be deployed by Xiang to create a reverse process, one of genetic renewal rather than destruction. There was only one problem. This third person would have been perfect for her to deploy the nanotech straight away and thus reverse the genetic degeneration of Nat and Dan. However, this person was useless to her. They had also been affected by the destructive process which would eventually kill the twins. This meant that there was another hybrid at imminent risk from this invasive and deadly genetic virus.

Had Xiang known that this very hybrid was about to eject somebody who was completely innocent from an airlock, she might have been slightly less concerned about their welfare.

CHAPTER THIRTEEN

Recollection

For a moment it was as if the past eighteen years had never happened. Here they were together once again, in the same place and under great duress and pressure. The simulation exercises had been carried out in space: this ship, the Quadrants, the entire project must have been conceived many years ago.

Simon always knew his work had been part of something big – and very top secret – but he'd never imagined it would be as far reaching as this. Both Kate and Simon had known real fear in this hangar. They'd been sure they were about to die, they'd seen the faces of family members streamed to these very screens and threatened with death. But it was the answer to that nagging question they'd carried with them for all these years that they were most pleased to have answered. The creature that had been in the corner when the simulation ended. It was not human, there was something off-world involved here. That explained a lot – particularly about the twins, and the amazing technology used in this place and in the Quadrants.

Kate looked at Simon. This memory and these strong emotions had helped her to refocus her mind after being under the influence of the neuronic device for so long. As the memories resurfaced, she was once again certain that she was experiencing her own thoughts here and not those of some remote and controlling force.

'So we've been here before,' said Simon, though he barely needed to say it.

'It looks exactly the same as it did then,' Kate picked up. 'It seems like it's been put in storage though.'

They'd both recognized immediately the distinctive rows of green grid lines which marked out this virtual reality arena.

'I wonder if it's still operational,' Simon thought aloud, making for the terminal where they'd seen the unusual figure sitting just before they were both shot unconscious. They'd thought it was for real at the time.

The terminal surged immediately to life as he moved deftly around the pads. This was standard Global Consortium navigation and configuration, he could probably figure it out.

Kate walked around the hangar exploring, looking for anything which might be useful. Suddenly she found herself in the middle of a warzone. Weapons were being fired, there were screams and yells, shells were exploding. It was battlefield hell.

Just as quickly it stopped.

'Whoa, sorry Kate!' Simon shouted across the hangar. 'It's working, it's programmed with a load of simulation exercises. This place renders immersive virtual reality environments – it's what happened to us in that exercise they sent us on. It all happened here, Kate. It wasn't real!'

Kate was severely shaken. It had felt immediately real. She wasn't sure she'd be able to hold her nerve if it happened again, even if she knew it was a simulation.

'I'm going to leave this activated,' Simon continued. 'It may come in useful later.'

Then Kate noticed something they'd both missed before.

Right along the length of the hangar, between the green grid lines, a narrow strip had been marked out, like a concealed pathway. It was faintly drawn along the floor, but definitely there.

'I want to try something, Simon.'

She ran to the end of the room and the beginning of the tramlines.

'Give me any simulation you want!' she shouted across the hangar.

Simon was in the same position where they'd noticed the alien figure eighteen years ago. It was unnerving for her. She saw him make some hand movements, then he was gone and she was immediately immersed in a new environment, only this time she understood that it was virtual. It was still frightening – the psychological trick was to disorientate, so you thought that one thing was happening, then it all changed in an instant.

Kate held her nerve, though all around her was a scene of mayhem, with explosions, bullets being fired and attackers coming at her. She walked a steady route through the hangar, keeping to where she knew the tramlines to be.

'Simon, turn it off, turn it off!' she shouted as she reached what she supposed must be near the end of the hangar.

The simulation stopped and the hangar returned. Simon was at the console, he'd seen everything on his monitor.

'You saw all that, I assume?' asked Kate. 'You can walk straight through this thing if you use that pathway, nothing touches you.'

'And did you notice the device in the ceiling?' he replied, nodding his agreement. 'That's central in every simulation, it's what they used to stun us in our own simulation exercise eighteen years ago.'

'This entire room is a psychological trick! This machine is meant to be beaten.'

They didn't know whether to be angry, amused or amazed at this new information. They certainly felt cheated: when they'd made their decision eighteen years ago, it had been in the heat of the moment, they'd genuinely thought that the lives of their family members were in danger. They hadn't known it was a simulation. Neither had they known they were in space.

Whatever they felt about the past, they would be thankful for this hangar later on. It would be the place which shielded them just before the end came.

The President's Plan

Mike tried to focus on the matter in hand. He forwarded a summary of the last file to Magnus. There were two Doctor Pierces, they were identical twins. That seemed to explain quite a bit. The man appeared to be everywhere, after all. But they were much more than ordinary twins. Like Dan and Nat, the Pierces were hybrids. That could be good or bad, he wasn't sure yet.

Mike reconsidered the circulation of the memo to only Magnus – he wondered if Xiang might find the information useful too. He copied her in, highlights only. If there were more hybrids like Dan and Nat it could help her to solve their current problem.

Mike was massively conflicted – he was learning things here that were explosive. He had direct access to intergovernmental secrets of the highest order. If he'd been under any less time pressure, he'd have quite happily sat there for days just reading all this stuff. But he was scanning – and he had to do so at extreme speed. There was no time to dwell on anything, he needed to read, assimilate and move on.

He and his team were sifting through clues which dated back many years. They were hoping to find a fragment which might help them to move forward against the constant threat of troopers launching their final assault on the bunker. It would surely come, it was only a matter of time. He had to get through as much of this data as he could before that happened – before they got trapped in the shootout that was heading their way.

Mike nearly skipped a file, thinking it was of no importance, but he jumped back. Its presence there jarred. He'd been a toddler when Ronald Reagan had announced his Star Wars defence programme, but as a teenager and a hacker it had been on his radar because it had moved into hacking folklore. If you could find the Global Defence Matrix and leave the government a little message? Well, that was the Holy Grail for the hacking community. However, nobody ever managed to find a trace of it. In fact, many hackers dismissed the project as propaganda, suspecting that the United States was using it as a tool to worry their political enemies. That was the only reason Mike returned to the file. He was curious. What was it doing there if the defence strategy was just a fiction created by an American president? He scanned the files – it was like a potted history of a famous project. He could see how it had been started by Reagan, renamed by Clinton, then mysteriously disappeared under Bush. During Bush's first term it had become a Global Consortium matter, taken out of the President's hands.

That must have been some decision to take. To think that all this stuff was going on and nobody knew. Everybody was blaming Bush for the Gulf War, while really there were far more sinister things going on right under their noses. As he read on Mike realized the enormity of what he was seeing. This was a global defence matter. It had moved beyond being just a tool for the United States many years ago. And they had succeeded too, they'd managed to create a complete defensive matrix around the entire planet. It could shoot down any nuke – they all had a detectable signature, and until they could remove that trace, they were all rendered pretty well useless.

Mike felt a moment of anger thinking about how terrifying the prospect of all-out nuclear war had been for his generation. He'd have liked to have known about this, why was it kept from the population? He read on, battling against his every instinct to become distracted. It was worth it – he found the information that he was after. He had to burrow deep down into the data to find it, but it was all there.

The full set of codes to activate the entire Global Defence Matrix were all held in that documentation. God forbid that any of Mike's old hacker chums would ever have found this.

Magnus would need to know about this straight away. Anything related to defensive or offensive processes was crucial now, especially with Quadrant 3 being the last remaining area to be free from sabotage. Mike sent the codes directly to Magnus, and he copied in Viktor too. The quiet and mysterious Viktor. Mike didn't know much about him yet, but he had to trust the process. Viktor was a Custodian. He'd been appointed to a leadership role by the Global Consortium – he needed to see this information, along with Xiang.

Time to move on. Mike forced himself away from the defence files and on to the next data-set. All around him, like summarizers on budget day, his tech team were sifting through these files, passing on anything that might be of strategic importance.

Mike was just opening up the next file when Magnus's face appeared on the screen at his console. He was worried and not making much effort to hide it.

'Mike, you need to come straight to the med lab. It's not good news, I'm afraid. It's Amy ...'

Identity

'Nat,' I whispered as loud as I dared, then remembered that I could try this telepathically now. Neither of us was used to communicating that way just yet, it was more instinctive to talk, but either way I got her attention.

She smiled when I showed her the comms tab. It hurt her though, her lip was cut and bleeding. Then I showed her the slip of paper. This got a much stronger reaction than the comms tab.

'Where did you get that!' she exploded.

I scrunched my face at her. Not quite telepathy, but a clear warning to keep her voice down. I'd never have placed myself in the position of wise and learned, but compared to Nat's impetuosity I was the model of maturity and careful consideration.

'We have a friend out there,' I replied.

I went on to describe him as best I could.

'It can't be Dae-Ho. He died. I was there.'

'You died and I was there!' I reminded her.

'Good point. If it is Dae-Ho, that's incredible, Dan. He's the one who helped me to escape from Pierce in the first place.'

Again, I got a glimpse of a story that still lay untold. Nat was away for three years – what had happened to her in that time? I'd been quick to condemn her rage and impatience, but I had no knowledge of what she'd been through since the day of the accident. Who was I to judge her?

'We need to get Dae-Ho and his friends out of here with us,' she resumed. 'They're being held against their will – their families have been threatened.'

I was getting a better sense of why Nat hated Pierce so much: everything he touched seemed to turn to something hateful or violent. I needed to get a message to Simon and I was also anxious to let Magnus know where we were. I was beginning to think better of sneaking off like that now – we should have told them where we were going. At least Mum knew what I was up to – sort of – she'd let everybody know when she got back to Quadrant 3. I had a pang of concern about Mum – was she okay? I'd barely had time to think about my family, things had been moving so fast.

We had to focus on what we knew and what we could control. That meant we had to get a message out before Pierce and his ugly alien pal discovered we had a comms tab. I decided to send a text to Magnus. He would be aware that something was happening with the Quadrants, but he'd have no idea about the existence of this place. How would he even find us up here in space?

Mum's sym node had stopped working when I left her earlier. It was only Nat and me who could get us up here. Into space. Simon and Kate were our best chance of escape – and perhaps this man called Dae-Ho. I told Magnus that the Pierces were twins too. Just like me and Nat. That might be useful information for Xiang.

We were really short on time now, maybe half an hour left until the nanovirus got us. I felt a moment of despair, as if it was time to give up, then I quickly rallied. It wasn't over yet – we would fight until our last breath. This wasn't only about me and Nat, it was about Mum, Dad and everybody else on Earth too.

I remembered that the comms tab should be carrying Xiang's data about the genetic destruction process that was going to kill Nat and me. When I saw the data projecting my remaining life expectancy, I caught myself tapping the comms tab. It had risen. I had longer to live. Some good news at last. According to the tab, I had a clear hour until the genetic breakdown process completed. Had I gained some time somewhere? I was nervous about these numbers, fearing they might be wrong because we were in space.

I looked up to see Henry Pierce and a group of troopers approaching us. This couldn't be good. I slipped the comms tab into my pocket before the first trooper grabbed me. Next they got hold of Nat and finally two troopers seized Harold Pierce by the arms. He was barely conscious – if they kept beating him like that, he'd be no use to anybody. Ahead I could see another trooper forcibly escorting one of Dae-Ho's friends along the corridor. Henry grabbed the terrified guy by his hair, threw him into the airlock and pressed the pad at the side of the door to close it. He keyed in a code and the far door of the airlock opened wide into space. Dae-Ho's friend was ejected in an instant. One minute he was there pounding on the door, the next he was a distant dot, lost in infinity. I was breathless with shock. I couldn't believe what he'd done.

Next it was my turn. Henry Pierce swung round to face me. He went straight for my pockets and pulled out the comms tab, then slammed my head against the wall. Jeez that hurt! My eyesight was blurred and my ears ringing from the force of the impact.

We were marched along the corridor and pushed into the centre of the ops area. It was still surrounded by the holographic faces on the small screens which lined the walls, but there was a larger panel too, a main screen on which we were looking at someone – or something – other worldly.

Zadra Nurmeen was chuckling to himself in the corner, they clearly had another bit of antagonism planned for us. I hadn't had a chance to take a proper look at him yet – I daren't take my eyes off Henry Pierce. I never knew when that man would strike next. Zadra Nurmeen had a human appearance overall, yet it was easy to tell he wasn't human at all. The number of fingers on his hands gave it away, of course, but it was more than that. He was smaller than everybody else here, but still powerful and warrior-like. He looked like he meant business. I certainly wouldn't pick an argument with him, that was for sure. His clothing was military, not like anything you'd ever see on Earth, and slung across his back he had a long, black sheath. I wasn't sure I wanted to know what he was concealing in there. Compared to Pierce, he was quiet and this made him immediately more threatening.

Pierce began to talk. I shifted my gaze to him.

'I calculate that you have about twenty minutes left before the nanovirus process is complete. So I need to know. Will you help me or not?'

I heard a moan from the floor beside me. Harold Pierce was coming round. His attention was immediately drawn by what was on the main screen.

'You have proven to me that the nanovirus process works well, but you twins are nothing to me now. I frankly don't care if you live or die.'

I'd remember to thank him for his good wishes later. I didn't like where this was heading.

'I want you to go to Zatheon and infect the entire population. You two can help us to land an even bigger prize than Earth.'

'Why would we want to do that?' challenged Nat.

Did she never learn? She needed to keep her mouth shut a bit more often.

'Because it's the only way you'll get to come out of this alive,' he replied, 'and meet your real mother.'

'I don't even believe that she's alive!' Nat shouted.

She started to run at him, only to be stopped by a trooper. She was pushed to the ground again, at the side of Harold Pierce who was now looking at the large screen. I followed his gaze. I wasn't sure what I was looking at – it resembled Frankenstein's monster. There was a woman's face in there – it looked human, but she had no hair and her skin was pale white, almost translucent. She was attached to a panel which seemed to be a cross between a computer and a life-support system. She was muttering wildly. Her eyes were shut, but her eyelids constantly flickered. I didn't know what I was looking at, but it was deeply distressing. Whoever that was on the screen seemed to be in a heightened state of wretchedness.

A tear dropped from Harold Pierce's eye as his brother moved into the centre of the ops area and gestured towards the large screen we were now all looking at.

'Twins, meet your mother!'

He laughed at us, like an evil magician who'd just pulled a dead rabbit out of a hat. 'Or the Queen as we like to call her. This is Davran Saloor, the supposed saviour of planet Earth.'

CHAPTER FOURTEEN

Recovery

Amy sat up on the med lab bed, itching to get away and throw herself back into the business of helping Dan and Nat. She'd just been on the receiving end of the same amazing technology that had saved her life after Simon shot her earlier in order to maintain his cover. It had healed her cuts and bruises right in front of her, accelerating the natural regeneration process, and although she was still stiff and sore, she was ready for action. Again. Besides, she needed to get that backpack over to Magnus and Mike – the trooper's helmet and the SD card might hold some crucial item of information.

Through the glass of her own cubicle, she could see the trooper who'd travelled with her in the transporter. She thought she'd been in a bad way after their altercation, but he was looking rough. He was restrained and under guard, but he was shaking and struggling. It looked to Amy like he was going cold turkey after an addiction – he seemed to be wrestling to get by without something that he was desperately craving. Amy wondered about the voices in the helmet, the ones that had been so meaningless and unbearable to her.

Her train of thought was broken as Mike burst through the med lab doors in a state of panic. He was immediately delighted and relieved to see his wife sitting up and quite clearly with her fire back.

'What on earth have you been up to?' he asked, rushing to hug her before breaking off to inspect her wounds. He was about to admonish her for running off like that into the heart of the trouble, but he stopped himself. They were all doing things that none of them would have dreamed possible only a week ago, himself included. And, although he was terrified for the lives of his family, if he was honest with himself, he loved the adrenalin rush of it all – it was an incredible, if terrible, experience.

He could see in Amy's face that she felt the same. Of course these events were horrifying, but the heightened senses let loose as a result of being in the thick of something like this? Well, it beat humdrum day-to-day life, even if the stakes were so high.

They ditched the chit-chat. They knew time was precious.

'How long do Dan and Nat have left?' Amy asked.

'We're not sure. Xiang sent a text update telling us she'd come across an anomaly and that it had extended their life expectancy by thirty minutes or so.'

'We must be on the last hour now ...'

That focused both of their minds once again. Forget the excitement, concentrate only on the problem.

'Mike, look, there are some things in that bag over there that might be useful.'

Mike walked over to the bag which had been thrown to the side by the med lab team.

The first thing he pulled out was Amy's laptop, he almost laughed.

'I'm not sure what use this old thing will be. Have you seen the tech I'm using in the control room?'

'Not the laptop,' replied Amy, a little impatient with the attitude, 'the helmet, take out the helmet.'

Mike struggled to get it out of the bag, but he immediately understood Amy's urgency when he saw what it was. The helmet was alive with digital circuitry. He held it to his ear. He could hear the mess of voices very faintly without having to put it on his head.

'This is out of my league, I need to pass this to Magnus.'

Amy got off the bed hesitantly – she wasn't sure her legs would hold her. They did, and she grabbed the clothes she'd been wearing during the struggle. They'd been neatly folded and placed alongside her bag, ready for when she recovered enough to leave the med lab. She fumbled in the pocket. A moment of panic. She couldn't find it. Another search. It was stuck in the corner of the pocket, only a small card, but still much larger than the micro SD cards most people had in their mobile phones. She handed it to Mike.

'Take this. When I first came across Nat she was trying to get some information off this using my laptop.'

Amy tried to recall those hazy memories of her first encounter with Nat in the car park. She could remember snippets, but no details of conversations or feelings. They had been suppressed by the device in her neck, the one that was now powerless to control her. Thanks to James. She stopped for a moment and her sadness returned. In the heat of a fight it was all too easy to forget about the people who'd lost their lives. They'd remember James later, the time to mourn would come. For now, it had to be about saving lives. Including Dan and Nat's.

Mike put the SD card in his pocket and picked up the laptop and helmet.

'Okay, I'll get on to this. You stay here and rest.'

He knew it was the wrong thing to say the minute the words left his mouth.

'Like that's going to happen!'

Amy was already activating the sym node on her hand.

'Before you go anywhere with that helmet, Mike, you're coming with me. I'm going to find Dan and Nat. And I'm not coming back again until I've got both of them ...' She paused, her eyes grew moist, but she was not one to cry easily. 'They're coming back with me, dead or alive.'

Cluster

The Helyion ship concealed below the surface of Lake Karachay had been emitting a pulse for some time now. It was encrypted, undetected. No other O-Fed members would even suspect that the Helyions were capable of this yet.

The inhabitants of Helyios 4 had been deceptive. What was the phrase they used on Earth? The Helyions loved this one: 'Never judge a book by its cover'. It didn't really translate that well into Helyion, but the gist of it was exactly right. Never be deceived by external appearances. To other, more socially advanced species, the Helyions were brutes, charmless, without manners and ungracious. They had to be, their existence was mineral based. You get what you're given when it comes to your home planet, and you have to make the best of it.

On Helyios 4 the rules were different – you can't make judgements on another planet's culture just because it doesn't align with your own. It's like the highly educated snobs who stick their noses up at the multi-millionaire who started life as a market stallholder. Never be deceived by origins. The Helyions were an extremely advanced race, in spite of appearances. They'd laughed at the hilarity of being spotted by other members of the Off World Federation who'd actually tracked an old trash disposal ship when they first believed the Helyions capable of space travel. They'd thought that was the Helyions' first foray into space travel.

The truth was that the Helyions had been travelling in space for many, many years. Their cloaking was more advanced than anybody else presently had access to in the Off World Federation. It turned out that the market stallholder knew a few tricks that the snobby entrepreneurs didn't.

So, when they were made members of O-Fed, as they'd shown themselves now capable of basic space travel, the whole thing had in fact been a big mistake. Or a terrible deception, it depended on how you looked at it. They'd based their entire judgement on spotting an old beat-up waste disposal ship. But it had offered the Helyions an excellent opportunity. They knew their planet was dying, that very fact was what had forced them out into space in the first place. The Off World Federation had brought to their attention a rather nice planet by the name of Earth. A planet that was also dying. A planet which could meet, largely speaking, all of the requirements of the Helyion population.

Here was a brilliant opportunity. Only, the Helyions

had no intention of going to war with the Off World Federation. There was no chance they could win against eleven adversaries. Their planet was small, their population relatively low, they were in no fit state for an intergalactic battle. However, the man Pierce had given them an excellent chance to solve their planet's problems. Zadra Nurmeen would goad this man's sociopathic madness. He'd administer a drugs cocktail similar to the one used on him as a child, the very drugs which had created his severe psychotic problems in the first place. They'd let this mad, evil genius destroy his own planet. Then they'd move in and take what was left, no warfare required.

The final tests had been done in Lake Karachay – this place was perfect for the cluster, a radioactive wasteland, part of the wonderful, mineral-rich land mass known as Russia to the humans. The first, cloaked ship was joined, one at a time, by other Helyion ships. There were twenty-nine of them in all, forming a sinister hub over the polluted lake. Nobody in the Off World Federation knew they were there. Neither did Henry Pierce have any knowledge of their presence. Who could tell what erratic actions he might have carried out if he'd seen that his only friend, Zadra Nurmeen, had been deceiving him – poisoning him – for all of those years?

There was one more ship to arrive. That final ship had an important job to do. It would be the cloaked ship that transported Zadra Nurmeen back to Earth after Pierce had set in motion the last, irreversible stage of the sabotaged terraforming process. This would be the final scorching of the Earth, Terra Level 3.

The Helyions were going to sit and wait until Pierce destroyed the planet. Then, under the terms of the Off

World Federation Covenant, they were going to claim the wreckage as their own.

Break Out

Simon and Kate had left a tracker on the door of the simulation area. Their plan was to draw the battle away from Dan and Nat to a place where they had the tactical advantage. They'd also located some useful props from that room, namely a few smoke canisters and a remote activation key for the simulations console. Handy equipment to be carrying, bearing in mind what they now had planned.

They made their way through the corridors of the Nexus, dodging the troopers who seemed to be growing in numbers all the time. Kate was feeling increasingly uneasy. She shuddered to think they'd been under her sole command when this day had started, and a dull, sickening sensation in her stomach halted her progress for a few moments.

'What is it?' asked Simon, sensing her unease.

'I just got this overwhelming feeling of guilt. I can't believe what I've done, I don't know how to make up for it.'

'We're at war, Kate. You were under somebody else's control. We can still sort this out.'

Kate knew he was right, and she picked herself up and carried on moving. But she resolved that, before this battle was over, she'd make up for the damage that she'd done, she was determined to set things straight. Even if that meant losing her own life doing it.

Simon put up his hand to urge her to silence. They were outside the main ops area. He could see Doctor Pierce. And there were the twins – Dan and Nat – their faces were white, they looked like they'd just received some terrible news. There was a man next to Dan and Nat. Simon struggled to make him out. He thought his eyes were playing tricks on him. It was a second Doctor Pierce.

At that moment, Simon got it. He didn't know the detail – he didn't need to – but it all made perfect sense. If there were two people identical in appearance – twins, clones, whatever they were – what happened that day must have been sabotage. The man he saw talking to the twins' mum as his car swerved at the girl, it must have been one of these men.

One of them must have had Global Consortium access, it just pieced together for him as he looked at the two of them. It had to have been how this whole deception was carried out. He'd always felt there seemed to be an extra person involved, like it didn't quite add up. It was easy to tell who was in charge here. One of the men looked bruised, beaten and weary, the other looked charged, confident and powerful.

And to the side him, sitting on a chair and smirking, somebody – or something – else. Kate had recognized him too. That was the thing that had been sitting at the control desk in the simulation area eighteen years ago. They'd been right, the creature they'd seen on that day had not been human.

Now they knew who the enemy was. And they now had a plan to break out their friends.

Face To Face

. . .

What do you do when the life you thought was yours turns out to be completely different? The sister I thought was dead was alive. We turned out to be aliens – or human–alien hybrids, to be more accurate. The man I thought had been sent to help me at school had turned out to be a brilliant scientist in charge of one of the most important challenges in the planet's history. And he had an identical twin who seemed hell-bent on destroying Earth. And now, to top it all, I was being introduced to my birth mother.

But this was no joyful reunion. She looked terrible. She was attached to wires and tubes, muttering furiously and looking wretched. It was disturbing to see. I turned away. But how could I turn away from the woman who was supposed to be my mother? I got an overwhelming sense of revulsion from Nat. She felt the same as me – whatever they'd done to her was horrible. Like most of the people in that room, she wasn't responsible for her actions. She needed our help.

Harold was clearly shaken by what we were looking at on the screen. Henry seemed to feel the need to explain himself.

'Your mother is currently issuing our instructions to the troopers. We hijacked her telepathic abilities.' Then he added, 'And thanks to you too, Nat, for helping us with that. We are very grateful for your help with our ... experiments.'

This telepathy thing was really strong in Nat and me now, and I could feel the surge of rage she experienced as he spoke. I was quick to urge her to caution. Nothing would be gained by goading this man, she'd only get herself hurt. Hurt more.

'To help focus your minds on my offer, you may like to know a few things,' Henry continued. 'We are about to set in motion the final stage of the terraforming process. This will destroy the planet and make it uninhabitable for all of the humans who live on it. They'll never wake up, the planet will burn as they slumber.'

At this, the holographic faces that surrounded the ops area started protesting, but we couldn't hear them. Pierce had silenced their speakers. Their protests could be seen, but not heard.

'We will also destroy the Nexus and the Quadrants – it's worked out pretty well this Unification process, it saves us having to destroy them on Earth.'

Then he added spitefully, 'Thanks for your help with that, Harold.'

'Why would we want to know this, you psycho?' Nat almost spat at him.

'Because there is going to be nothing left for you to return to. Earth will be destroyed, this ridiculous ark which was built by the Global Consortium will be destroyed, and the Off World Federation will see this as a terrible accident, a pioneering project gone wrong. My friend here, Zadra Nurmeen, will file a formal claim for custodianship under the Covenant and he and I will become legal owners of your dead planet.'

I urged Nat to calm down. Earlier I'd thought her more battle-ready than me, but now all I saw was recklessness. She really needed to think things through more carefully.

'And what about Davran?' asked Harold Pierce. He had finally rallied and wanted answers about his friend – our mother.

'We don't really need her for much longer,' his brother replied. 'We're moving all of the troopers up here now, into the outer sections of the Nexus. We'll destroy them when we blow up the Nexus.'

The troopers around us didn't flinch when he said this.

He'd just announced they were all going to be blown up in space, but it didn't seem to have registered with any of them. I reminded myself that they weren't really part of this, they were being controlled by Henry Pierce and his alien friend.

The face of the woman on the screen – our mother – told it all. She might have been controlling these troopers because of some villainy Pierce had committed, but her sense of right and wrong must still have been very much intact. She was commanding those troopers in spite of herself – she was struggling to stop every evil instruction that was forced upon her, but she was losing that battle. Whatever those tubes and wires were doing, they were compelling her into actions she didn't want to execute. That must have been why she looked so anguished. It must have been a terrible thing to be carrying out atrocities and unable to stop yourself. A living torture.

Nat was right, Pierce was a monster.

My mind had wandered off while he was speaking. I needed to listen. We needed to get this information back to Magnus.

'What about Davran?' Harold Pierce asked again. He must have really cared about our mother, he was deeply concerned about her. I really hoped I'd get to know her.

'She'll just burn out,' laughed Henry. 'By the time the troopers go offline, her mental capacities will be exhausted. She'll just be a shell .... and you know the laws about ostracism, Harold.'

I didn't like sound of that.

'What does that mean?' I spoke directly to Harold. Nat turned to hear the answer.

'When you're ostracized, you're there forever,' he replied. 'The *ISOC*ells are wired to make sure it's permanent. They've managed to locate her *ISO*Cell, I don't know how, and they've somehow got a transporter onto it. Nothing surprises me about these two, they had enough access to Genesis 2 to be able to do these things. There's just one problem with the *ISO*Cells ...'

Here it was. I was getting used now to detecting when bad news was coming.

'They were never supposed to be boarded, but that's just covenant law. Henry and Zadra Nurmeen won't care about the risks of being ostracized themselves. But when the prisoner dies, the *ISO*Cell explodes, there's no trace left, they live in isolation until that happens.'

Okay, so far so good, that didn't sound pleasant, but it wasn't too bad. It was like a funeral in space.

'Nobody is ever supposed to leave those things,' he continued, seeing the urgency for more information on our faces. 'When the last live person tries to exit the *ISO*Cell, it will explode. Davran is stuck there – if they destroy the transporter, she's lost and isolated in space, we'll never find her. If she tries to leave the *ISO*Cell, it'll explode, and that'll be the end of it ...'

Harold's words were left hanging as Henry charged up to him and pounded him in the head with his bloody knuckles.

CHAPTER FIFTEEN

Signals

Xiang looked at her screens. A fourth data stream had just appeared. From nowhere. This was all new to her. She shuddered to think what was going on wherever Dan and Nat were right now.

She'd received Dan's text alert about there being two Pierce brothers, and she knew now what that third data stream had been. One of the Pierces. But if there was a new nanovirus host now, what did that mean? This genetic destruction, whatever its source, was being passed on between hybrids. How though?

She didn't know yet but as the latest information feed had come online, she'd immediately seen the hazard levels for Dan, Nat and whichever Pierce hybrid had been affected first reduce immediately. They seemed to be dealing with it like a committee – as a new hybrid was infected with the nanovirus, it seemed to help the others. It was as if this hybrid species was linked in some way, like they could actually help each other to survive longer. The scientist in her knew this would be an incredible evolutionary concept. Xiang felt immediately guilty for even daring to be excited about the prospect of running more tests on Dan and Nat – if they got out of this thing alive.

For now, they'd just bought themselves a little more time. But as far as she knew, there were no more hybrids. That meant that when this destructive genetic killer attained viral levels of 100 percent, all four hybrids would be dead.

And by her reckoning, the most time any one of them had to survive was just over one hour.

Transported

Mike and Amy walked up to the elevator on the first floor of the bunker. It was heavily armed and the explosives teams were getting very jittery. They knew that whatever move would be made to take over this structure must play out soon.

When Amy walked towards them, they knew what she was up to, and they moved aside to let her get through.

'I'll need you to stay close with the helmet for the sym node to work,' Amy reminded him. 'Just make sure it works before you leave the area.'

Mike grabbed her and hugged her.

He was so proud of his wife, immensely impressed by what she was doing, and he feared that he might lose her in whatever was going to happen next.

'It's okay,' she said. 'We need to take care of our kids,

Mike. You do your thing with the tech – I'm going up there to kick some ass!'

He smiled and released her from his embrace.

She walked into the elevator and pressed the new symbol that had appeared since the Nexus had come online. This was where Dan was heading – it was a wild chance, but hopefully this symbol would activate the transporter and take her to him. The doors closed and she pressed the new touchpad. The elevator jolted, but nothing happened. She tried again, but again nothing happened.

'Damn it!' she cursed, kicking the side of the elevator, just missing one of the packs of explosive which were stacked up there in case of trooper attack.

Amy decided to try the symbol one more time – it was useless for her to try to head anywhere else, she needed to follow Dan's lead. This time it worked. The transporter fired up, the elevator interior lit up, and she was immediately transported to the same place as Dan.

Act Of Rebellion

The small remaining conscious part of her mind could sense what was going on. She'd known immediately that the trooper had been wounded and his helmet removed. She'd become aware of that as soon as the woman had placed the helmet on her own head.

At any one time she was processing hundreds of pieces of data. And now she could sense that this woman was trying to use a sym node ... to get to the Nexus. But this woman was not a trooper, she was the enemy. Wasn't she?

The small part of humanity that still functioned within

her told that this woman could mean help. Salvation even. The Queen was fighting with every last drop of will that she could summon, but she was losing the battle, she was under Pierce's deadly control.

But then she detected the woman trying to activate the transporter on Quadrant 3. This woman could help her. She was not the enemy, perhaps she was a final chance of escape? She tried desperately to activate the sym node authorization when the woman first touched the activation pad in the elevator.

At the same time, hundreds of pieces of information cycled through her brain – from the troopers, the Nexus, the Quadrants and from Doctor Pierce – and she urged herself to separate this information. She failed. The woman had tried again.

The Queen forced herself to fight the thing that compelled her against her will. She was losing her energy now, she knew that she was dying.

Then, a final chance, the woman had tried to use the sym node a third time. She was persistent. The Queen commanded every last bit of free will that she could muster, and for a split second she was Davran once again. And in that moment she gave Amy access to the Nexus via the transporter in Quadrant 3. It was a last act of rebellion from somebody who could no longer fight the evil that had been done to her.

It was a desperate grasp at freedom, a final chance to escape the terrors to which she'd been subjected by her torturers.

Obsolete

. . .

Mike listened to the sound of the transporter taking his wife to wherever she was heading and he made his way back to the control room.

A text update from Xiang told him that they'd just been granted a little more time to save Dan and Nat. About an hour he reckoned. An hour is such a short time normally, but now it was a matter of life and death for his children.

There had to be something on this SD card, why else would Nat have been so interested in it? Where was she now? And Dan? Damn these comms tabs, there was no sign of the twins. At least they'd sent a text message, they were still alive. For now.

Mike delivered the helmet to Magnus, explaining what it was, and headed back to his work area. His tech team had nothing to report, just more files, more snippets of information, including interesting notes about Dan, written by Harold Pierce, about his difficulties after Nat's death.

Pierce knew exactly what it was. He'd already experienced 'the disconnect', as it was known among the Zatheons. Although he hadn't been able to share his own experience with Dan or his parents at the time, he knew that what Dan was going through was entirely normal. He'd had to endure it – as had his brother – and so had Davran when she'd left her own sister. The symbiotic bond could bring so much strength, but at times it also brought terrible pain.

There were a few more random notes the team had flagged up, all very interesting, but nothing which helped to move things on. It turned out from a personal diary log that Harold Pierce's tie had been a gift from Davran Saloor. She'd had it made from a Zatheon textile which had amazing properties. It was thin, light, beautiful to touch – yet extremely tough. The Zatheons used the textile for many things, including heavy industrial purposes. Davran Saloor had given it to Doctor Pierce as a sign of friendship, because of the compassion and care he'd shown to her while on Earth. She'd have loved the Zatheons to work more closely with Earth, the two species had so much to learn from each other, but the elders had resisted. Davran wanted Harold Pierce to know how much she cherished his friendship.

But of course the tie had deep scientific significance as well. She'd added something unique to the tie, a token of trust and kinship. The symbol on the tie, which had amused and distracted Dan so much at his sessions with Doctor Pierce, would change colour whenever a Zatheon was nearby to let them know they were in the presence of a member of the same species. This is what Dan had seen, it had been the coloration that had intrigued him. If only he'd known back then that his birth mother was giving him a message. She was telling him that Harold Pierce was a friend.

Mike sifted the new data and discarded it swiftly, it could all wait for later, it meant absolutely nothing to him, neither would it help the twins. He took the SD card out of his pocket and started searching his terminal for a slot to plug it into.

'You're kidding?' he cursed to himself.

He called over to Jen from the tech team.

'Jen, where are the card slots in these things?'

'Don't need them, don't use them!' she replied. 'It's dead technology.'

This place was so hi-tech, they'd moved well beyond these old devices. Mike had encountered this issue already. It's how he'd accessed the files they were searching, they'd been encrypted using old coding systems.

He dared to wonder if this was the same thing again, crucial data hidden in plain sight on old systems. Almost defunct technology which any decent geek would dismiss out of hand. But how was he going to access it? Of course! He had Amy's laptop with him in the rucksack. It's what Nat had been trying to use to get to the data herself. He thrust his hand into the bag and drew out the laptop which he'd dismissed so readily when he'd been speaking to Amy in the med lab. He regretted that now. This old thing might hold the solution. He put the SD card in the slot, fired up the PC and got ready to see what information Nat had been so keen to read.

Secure Connection

In all the commotion Zadra Nurmeen had slipped away unnoticed. He'd not gone far, but he knew the patterns of behaviour with Pierce: he'd get angry, start ranting, hit or kick somebody – or both – and then do something unpredictable.

Nobody noticed that he was gone, except for Dae-Ho, who was dutifully attending to the task assigned to him. Keeping his head bowed, moving slowly but steadily, desperately trying not to provoke the man who'd terrorized him and his friends for so many years, and who had sent a good friend out to perish in the airlock.

Zadra Nurmeen left the ops area for only a few minutes, but Dae-Ho saw it all from his console. He was speaking to somebody and he didn't want Pierce to know.

Dae-Ho was too far away to hear what was being said, but he got the sense of what was going on. Zadra Nurmeen was hatching a plan. And it didn't appear to include Henry Pierce.

Overheard

Simon and Kate had been about to make a move when the alien had left the room unannounced, heading straight for them.

They'd flinched as Henry Pierce's fist had slammed into his brother's bloody head and they saw that the alien had taken this violence as his cue to make a sharp exit. They hung back in the shadows watching him as he started talking to somebody, but it was in his own tongue, they could only make out snippets. It was almost comedic, every now and then they'd hear a word they recognized – like 'Pierce' – for which there was no alternative word in his own language.

Simon and Kate didn't need to translate to get the gist of what was going on. They only had to read the body language. The conversation was hushed and collusive. Something was being planned. The alien kept glancing at Pierce to make sure his absence had not been noticed. Whatever was being said was not meant to be heard by anybody else.

But it was the final two words that both Simon and Kate recognized and would transmit back to Magnus minutes later when the alien had returned to his seat, still unnoticed by a furious Henry Pierce. Those two words were 'Lake Karachay'.

CHAPTER SIXTEEN

A Sinister Address

My mind was working furiously – Pierce seemed to have all the exits blocked and I couldn't think what to do next. We wouldn't be able get Davran, our birth mother, off the *ISO*Cell because then it would self-destruct. We couldn't replace her with somebody else. The chances were they'd never be found again – there was only one way to access it and that was via the single transporter link Henry Pierce and Zadra Nurmeen had set up.

The place was swarming with troopers. They were moving out of the bunkers and into the Nexus – meeting at this big, sinister nest in space. It was a hornet's nest too. Virtually everything here could give a nasty sting.

I'd lost track of how long Nat and I had to live. We could disappear in a puff of smoke any minute. I didn't know what would happen when our time was up. How long did we have left now?

I tried to focus. Everything I'd achieved since the

bunker doors closed on me for the first time had been done through strategy and planning. I needed to look around at what was available, what I could use. I could see our comms tabs and weaponry placed on a work area to my side, but the troopers were all around us and there was no chance of getting to it. I'd also seen a makeshift contraption towards the back of the room. I had a hunch that I knew what it was for.

Harold Pierce was out cold again on the floor. Nat was unusually quiet. For once she seemed to be using her brain, trying to figure out a way to break this impasse. Henry Pierce was about to get back into full flow. I doubted there was anything he could tell us that would surprise us, but still I bet he had a few tricks up his sleeve. Zadra Nurmeen caught my eye. He'd slipped out somewhere while all the commotion was going on. I wondered what he'd been up to. Henry Pierce broke my train of thought. He'd got that look in his eyes again and I braced myself for whatever was about to come.

'I have one last incentive to help you make up your minds about joining my little project on Zatheon,' he began, with a horrible smirk that confirmed it wouldn't be good news. 'I need to make sure that I also have the full attention of our friends on Earth for this one.' He was now addressing the holographic images of the world's leaders whose projections circled this ops area. 'We'll also need our friends from the bunkers to be patched into this announcement.'

He nodded to his alien pal, who pressed a few switches on the console to his side.

'Everybody hearing this?'

He got the confirmation he was after and took a deep breath, like an orator preparing to address the crowd. They didn't seem to have anybody from the bunkers up on the screens, so I assumed he was doing what Harold did earlier when he addressed the bunkers via the main PA systems. Which means Mum, Dad, Magnus, Viktor ... everybody should have been hearing this. Including Simon and Kate. What had happened to them? It was about time they showed their faces.

He started to speak.

'I'd like to begin by announcing to Quadrant 3 that I have good news for you – and bad news. The good news is we are presently evacuating the three Quadrants on Earth that we control and within the next ten minutes all of our trooper friends will have joined us here in beautiful space, in the Global Consortium's Nexus. The bad news is, we have everything you might want to save docked to this hub right now. The Consortium's little ark plan worked very well.'

He smiled and surveyed the faces of the world's leaders.

'I'd like to thank you all for sanctioning Unification – it will make it a lot easier to blow up the Nexus all at once, so my eternal gratitude for that rather bad decision.'

Harold Pierce was waking up again now, and by the look on his face, he'd rather have stayed out cold. The voices of the world's leaders were on mute, but I could guess what they were trying to say just by looking at the screens.

'In fact, I'd like to thank the Custodians of the bunkers for their help too. Like our lovely leaders, you have given us some great support today.'

Zadra Nurmeen turned around and pressed some buttons on his console. A trooper took an E-Pad handed to him by Zadra Nurmeen and headed towards Nat. She attempted to struggle but another trooper came up behind her and restrained her. Between the two of them, they forced Nat's hand onto the E-Pad and it gave a beep. The same then happened to me. I tried to resist, but I didn't have the strength to stop them placing my hand on the E-Pad. Another beep. Pierce waited for them to finish, then resumed what he was saying.

'Earlier today Xiang, Magnus and Viktor sanctioned the launch of the nuclear submarines and Dan and Nat kindly set that process in motion. We could not have done it without you, and I'd like to thank you for your help just now ...'

Here it came. What had we done?

'Twins, you have just launched two hundred nuclear missiles to a series of destinations programmed in by me. Those nuclear missiles are targeted at all four bunkers, which is why our trooper friends no longer need to stick around. Magnus and Viktor, I apologize, but I have over-ridden the preliminary coordinates set in by you. How naughty of you to target the other Quadrants, did you think you'd have to blow us out of the ground to beat us?'

He threw his head back and laughed. I thought only baddies on cartoon shows did that.

'We have also targeted some key installations around the globe, just to make extra sure that the planet is left with no viable form of government. The White House, the Houses of Parliament, the Kremlin, Zhongnanhai ... they'll all be gone within the hour. So if I were all of you, I'd start to do whatever it is you'd like to do, before it's all over. The terraforming sequence has been programmed in. Even if we hadn't launched the nukes, there would be no habitable planet left for you in fourteen days once Terra Level 3 was complete. And I'd like to thank the lovely Davran Saloor for that information. Dan and Nat, your mother kindly yielded the technical data we needed to mess up Terra Level 3 – so you've all been very helpful.'

He paused for effect, then broke out into that horrible smile of his.

'So we're doing you a kindness really.'

I didn't like the way he used the word 'yielded'. I could only guess at what horrible things he did to extract that information from Davran. Our mother.

'Oh, and Dan and Nat just set off the self-destruct sequence for the Nexus too – we'll be departing shortly on a Helyion ship to leave you all to it. So really, this is just a message to say farewell and wish you well. The first nuclear weapon will hit its target in roughly thirty minutes' time.'

For a second we were all completely stunned. Then all hell let loose. The ops area filled with smoke. Suddenly we were in Bedlam.

Fragmented

Simon and Kate had heard enough. They'd learned everything they needed to know to act. Pierce had sabotaged the nukes, everybody was on the final countdown and it didn't matter now what form their resistance took, anything was better than nothing. It was the endgame for everybody, there was nothing to lose.

They set off the smoke canisters procured from the simulation area, then began to shoot randomly into the air. They wanted to create as much confusion as possible, they were busting out Dan and Nat. Kate knew that even if she was going to die on this day, the single thing she would need to achieve would be to get the twins out alive, they were the only way this situation could be reversed now. She needed to atone for her sins, she was struggling to get to grips with the things that she'd done while under the control of the monster, Pierce.

It all happened very quickly. She rushed in to where she knew Nat was located. She took her by the arm and shouted 'Come with me!'

Simon ran towards where Dan had been, but he wasn't there. Through the dense smoke, Simon caught a glimpse of him. He seemed to have a purpose. Simon called to him, but in the commotion of troopers, weapon fire and shouting, he lost him. Kate called over to ask for help with Harold Pierce who'd been caught in the crossfire. He was wounded, but just about able to walk.

It was like the most dangerous game of musical chairs ever had just taken place. When the smoke began to clear, everybody was in a different place. Dan had used the diversion to grab a comms tab and make for the makeshift platform at the back of the ops area. He had a plan of his own.

Kate, Simon, Nat and Doctor Pierce were making their way along the corridor in a confusion of laser fire. Loud alarms were sounding throughout the Nexus – they had been dropped into a terrible battle scene in just a matter of minutes. It didn't matter though. They were fighting for their lives now. And for the lives of everybody on Earth.

Simon and Kate had the tracker. They were heading for the simulation area. On the way they were going to drop off Nat and Harold Pierce in the transporter, sending them back to Quadrant 3. Dan should have been with them – they would try to rectify that later, once they'd dealt with the troopers. They made their way through the corridors, using the remaining smoke bombs to confuse and separate the troopers at every intersection.

They successfully bundled Nat and Pierce into the transporter.

'Be careful when you exit,' warned Simon. I'll send a message over the comms tab to let them know you're coming.'

With Nat and Doctor Pierce safely dispatched, they set about executing the final part of their plan: to lure the troopers to the final battleground. This is where combat would take place, at a time and place of their choosing. This is where Simon and Kate would either win victory over the troopers or lose their lives trying.

Nuked

A chill ran through Viktor's body. He knew this scenario well, he'd been here before. The final move on the chessboard, the one which won the game or ended in defeat. This was why he'd held back those fifty nukes. A quick look at his E-Pad confirmed that Pierce had only got the first two hundred, his backup plan was still undetected. Fifty nukes at his fingertips – but where would he send them?

Like everybody else in the four bunkers, he'd listened to Henry Pierce's announcements in horror as they were broadcast throughout both levels of the bunker. Pierce was in space, what could he do? The fifty nukes were no use there.

But Viktor now knew one thing for sure. The codes that Mike had sent him for the Global Defence Matrix were going to be used for real for the first time. By Viktor Gorbunov. And on that day.

When he set that project in motion, President Ronald Reagan could never have imagined that it would be used in a scenario such as this one. Within the next fifteen minutes

Viktor was going to have to learn how to use this matrix, target the nukes and blow them out of the skies before they started to hit their destinations. Fifteen minutes was the time it would take the first of those deadly weapons to launch and land on his own bunker in Crimea. It was all the time he had before his own people would start to perish under the reign of terror that was about to fall across the planet.

Viktor steeled himself and calmed his mind. He'd need complete focus and concentration as he moved the final pieces of this chess game into position.

Confusion

When the doors opened and Amy looked out onto the deck of the Nexus, she was immediately disorientated. She almost stepped out into a swarm of troopers, but she managed to sneak out of the transporter unseen and hide.

She'd heard the announcement over the loudspeaker system and realized they were now into the final minutes. Whatever happened, whoever won, it would all soon be resolved. Then came the shriek of the alarms, smoke was drifting everywhere and the troopers began to move in one direction. Something had happened to put this place on full alert. She knew this was her opportunity. She'd come here to find Dan and Nat. She followed behind the troopers. They weren't aware of her – or bothered about her – whatever they were dealing with was taking precedence.

They quickly arrived in the central area of the spaceship. The smoke was dense and debilitating, but every now and then it would waft and clear and she'd get a glimpse of what was going on. In the haze, she thought she saw Dan. She was sure that she caught sight of Simon too.

'Dan?' she called, and he looked up. It was him, he was trying to get some contraption working, but he seemed to be struggling. She rushed over towards him, relieved to see him alive, desperate to get him out of this place.

As she grabbed his arm ready to embrace him, a stunning array of lights appeared around them and they were transported to a new destination. Location, unknown.

Mistaken

As the smoke began to clear in the ops area, the scene of carnage became clearer and clearer to those still there. There were several bodies on the floor, mostly Dae-Ho's friends who'd been caught in the crossfire. A horrible end to their miserable lives as slaves of Henry Pierce, and doubly sad as they were so close to achieving their freedom. There were troopers wounded and killed too, not many, but lives had been lost on both sides.

Zadra Nurmeen was nowhere to be seen, he appeared to have played no part in this battle. Like the opportunist he was, he'd left the fighting to the troopers, he had everything he needed to take care of his own interests for now. He simply exited the area, dragging Harold Pierce along with him as he did so, and taking refuge in the airlock area along the corridor. Within the past hour this had been a source of terror, fear and threat, but for him it was now a place of safety and refuge.

Only, when the commotion died down and Zadra Nurmeen returned to the ops area with a dazed and bloodied Harold Pierce, they were not walking as colleagues or equals might do, side by side. Zadra Nurmeen threw Harold into the room, indicating to the troopers to contain him should he try to escape.

As Harold Pierce recovered from the fall and turned around to face Zadra Nurmeen, he revealed an unusual tie. A tie that had once been a gift from a very good friend who'd been born on another planet.

Glimmer

Xiang was all ready to go. She'd set up a transfusion area in the med lab – this was where Dan and Nat would be saved if they got their breakthrough, or at least where she could extend their lives a little longer. But now she needed a hybrid, she couldn't progress anything until she had a live subject to work on. She needed Dan or Nat – or one of the Pierce twins.

She'd modelled a solution on her E-Pad, but she was missing some essential data. There was some key genetic information that she hadn't been able to piece together, a genetic code sequence which would enable her to deliver specially adapted nanotechnology via the spinal column. At the same time, she needed to carry out a blood transfusion and that would need to be with hybrid blood. Preferably uncontaminated blood.

Her E-Pad simulations indicated that although the hybrids' bodies contained an element of human DNA and blood, it was the alien blood type that was dominant. She hadn't even been able to think about what might happen if the hybrids had different blood types, as humans do – it would be 'game over' if that was the case. She was simply out of time.

She needed Dan and Nat in that med lab as soon as possible or she could settle for one of the Pierces. There was even a glimmer of hope now that the twins' real mother Davran was accessible, but that seemed so unlikely. That one was a long shot.

Her thoughts were disturbed by an alert on her comms tab. It was Magnus. He'd had his teams analysing the trooper helmet Amy had retrieved. He wanted Xiang to run a test on the trooper who was presently restrained in the med lab. They'd got an ID on him. Mike had cross-referenced the data with the Global Consortium records that he'd been able to access so far. They needed Xiang to check his DNA against her own records.

As far as they could tell, they'd found Dan and Nat's natural father.

Disappeared

As Simon pushed Nat and Pierce into the transporter, Nat slammed her hand on the unusual symbols and began the transportation process. The coloured lights began to activate immediately and she knew they were on their way to Quadrant 3. Relative safety at last. But without Dan. Damn it, they'd lost Dan in the confusion.

She struggled to find connection with him, she got glimpses of him, but nothing certain or lasting. They were still getting used to this telepathy thing – whatever it was between them – so it was a bit erratic. She saw that he was okay, he had a plan. He'd conveyed to her that she needed to get back to Xiang, to try to solve whatever was going to kill them. If the nukes didn't fall first. Yes, Dan had work to do. She wished she was with him, but she'd been set on a different path by Simon and Kate's rescue attempts. She'd have to leave it to Dan – to trust him.

Something had been unsettling her as the elevator transported back to Quadrant 3. She'd been looking at Doctor Pierce – distracted by her thoughts while she'd been thinking about Dan – but not particularly registering him.

He was wounded and stunned, but there was something about him that wasn't right. He didn't have the head wounds that Harold Pierce had had. And he wasn't wearing that tie.

She was in the elevator with Henry Pierce.

There had been a switch somehow – or Simon had grabbed the wrong Pierce in all of the confusion. She was stuck in a space the size of a closet with the man who had tortured and tormented her for over three years.

This was the opportunity for revenge that she'd stayed alive for.

CHAPTER SEVENTEEN

ISOCell (T minus 54 minutes)

I caught a moment to breathe. I think it worked. I'd never felt such a rush of adrenalin. I was terrified but exhilarated at the same time – it was a bizarre combination of wanting to run away and hide, yet not wanting to miss the action.

I took a leap of faith when the smoke filled the ops area. It must have been Simon and Kate. It was about time too. I knew they were probably trying to bust us out, but I had other plans. And this one I wanted to carry out on my own. If we still had some time left before everything started to go up in flames, well I wasn't going to sit there twiddling my thumbs. There was no way I was leaving our mother on that *ISO*Cell to die alone. Who can you rely on if you can't rely on your family? And I was her family now.

I'd been thinking back to when I was stuck alone in the bunker entrance when the sirens first went off. I didn't recognize that Dan. There was no way I'd just sit there now, waiting for somebody to come and rescue me. The cavalry perhaps? If I'd taken things into my own hands a bit more in the first place I might have been able to stop some of these events happening. No more would I just sit there waiting for stuff to play out around me. This was the new Dan – the one who took a crazy chance that a hunch might just pay off and he'd be able to beam to some mystery location deep in space and rescue his real-life alien mother.

Okay, it sounded mad to me when I said it to myself like that, but what other choice was there? I was seeing this thing through to the end. I wasn't going to sit there scared and powerless. This situation would play out anyway, with or without me.

There was a problem though. I'd planned on doing this thing alone and then Mum popped out of the smoke, just like that, and I'd suddenly got a companion. I'd intentionally kept Nat out of this, her temper kept landing us in deep trouble. I thought she was amazing but I needed a level head for what I was about to do.

'Where did you come from, Mum?'

I gave her a hug. I don't think I've ever appreciated my family so much. I was so glad to see her.

'It's a long story, Dan, but we need to move fast. You haven't got long left now.'

I'd grabbed my comms tab before running for the contraption at the back of the ops area. I took it out of my pocket. I knew I'd lost track of time, but I was shaken to see how long I had left before this genetic problem killed me. Fifty-four minutes. That number seemed to have gone up and down every time I'd looked at it, but it stared me in the face now. Less than one hour to save my own life and Nat's too.

And there were the nukes as well – there was no knowing how soon they would start to fall. It was almost overwhelming, but I calmed myself. One thing at a time. Each person would do their job. Trust that process, Dan, do your bit, hope that everybody else hits their own deadline.

I needed to speak to Magnus. I called him on my comms tab and he responded straight away – he patched me in to Dad, Simon, Viktor, Kate and Xiang. I think they call it a conference call in the business world, but I'll bet no corporation ever had an agenda like ours. The reception was terrible – it was hard to make out what was being said. Wherever we were, it must have been very deep in space. I couldn't even see the sun. I was no expert on space exploration, but shouldn't there have been a sun here? Somewhere?

We needed to get this done fast. I wasn't sure the signal would hold.

Magnus was good. He was obviously watching the clock – just like everybody else – and he brought us up to speed in a couple of minutes. I then quickly explained how I managed to transport to the ISOCell – at least that's where I thought I was. Pierce and his alien chum must have had a way to get to the ISOCell and it had to have been portable if nobody was supposed to find or visit Davran once she'd been banished.

I'd taken a chance. I hoped I was right. We were still in space, I could see that through the windows, and we were in a different place now. It had to be the ISOCell. My plan was to rescue Davran and to get all of us out without exploding the place. How I'd do that, I'd figure out later – first thing: find Davran.

Xiang was excited by this. She said that if we rescued Davran she'd be able to save me and Nat. It was exactly what she needed, some uncontaminated alien blood which she could use for a transfusion. She wasn't sure how she'd do it yet, but that was going to be her priority.

Simon and Kate rushed off before we'd even finished talking. They were going to lure the troopers into a trap. Then they'd try to finish off Henry Pierce and Zadra Nurmeen. They'd asked Magnus to check out Lake Karachay to see if it was of any significance. Magnus was working on the trooper helmet, he thought he was on to something. Viktor was tracking the nukes. He only had minutes left before the first one struck. Dad and his team were trying to sort out some SD card that Nat was carrying. They thought there might have been something useful on it.

And that was when we realized that someone crucial was missing from this meeting. Simon had told us that she was on her way with Harold Pierce, but she hadn't arrived yet. Where was Nat?

As if that wasn't enough, Mum and I had a new problem. Our comms tabs just died and we couldn't hear anybody. We were on our own.

Access

Mike returned to the SD card. He'd been distracted by Magnus's request to cross-check some data he'd retrieved from the trooper's helmet. At first he'd cursed the interruption, then he became completely absorbed in finding the information Magnus needed. He reckoned that if he was right they might be able to save Dan and Nat with the help of this trooper – this man.

Magnus was right. It had taken Mike some time, but he'd referenced the records and confirmed the theory. This part-man, part-machine was the first trooper. He was the original model. And his records had been altered. Clumsily, as it turned out, which probably meant there had been tampering. His records dated back to 2003. It seemed a bit hazy as to how he'd got involved. As far as Mike could see, the troopers had been assembled from teams of mainly military personnel who'd successfully completed a series of special tests. From the little that Amy had managed to tell him about what she and James had been involved with before they married, it did occur to Mike that she might have narrowly escaped this same process.

He was appalled to see that the troopers had been issued false death certificates. As they'd passed the tests – whatever they were – they'd had faked military deaths and had, quite literally, been removed from their everyday lives, to become a living army, kept in stasis. All achieved using cyber technology procured and adapted from a company called Magnum Enterprises. Mike struggled with his anger, he'd stumbled across yet another outrage connected with this project. Had these troopers given their consent to this? Their families thought they were dead, yet all this time they'd been alive.

Then he found it. The reference was JB BLP/0786. The 'J' stood for Jeff. The 'B' didn't seem to be important to anybody. But he'd been part of a cover up. Jeff wasn't even supposed to be part of this project. He was supposed to have been ostracized, whatever that meant – Mike didn't know. Jeff had appeared from nowhere, it seemed. He certainly hadn't been a part of the selection tests. Neither did he have a death certificate: his removal from life on Earth didn't appear to be a problem. For anybody.

It was only when Mike cross-referenced the data with a seemingly unrelated incident that had occurred around the same time that he made this particular sum add up. Dan and Nat's mother was called Davran Saloor. She'd had a relationship with a man called Jeff, which had been forbidden. Davran Saloor had been banished somewhere, and that's what was supposed to have happened to Jeff too. Instead, he'd been spirited away. He'd been placed in stasis for several years. He'd been adapted for use as a trooper using a new technology created by Magnum Enterprises. He'd been the first trooper.

None of that mattered, not now. There was only one thing that counted in that mass of information, in spite of the evil that had been inflicted on this man. He was Dan and Nat's natural, human father. He could save their lives. And he was lying there in the med lab right at that moment.

The Thirtieth Ship

Zadra Nurmeen prowled through the ops area as if he were the King of the Jungle. He owned this place, it was now his domain. He was quick to take control.

He sent updated objectives directly to the Queen who cascaded them immediately to the troopers: hunt down the escapees and kill on sight; terminate all humans on board, including the twins, but bring their spines back, he'd need those. They would contain enough genetic data to take out the Zatheon population when the time was right.

He then contemptuously turned off the holographic screens projecting the faces of the world's leaders. He didn't require their presence any more. As far as he was concerned, they were now dead. In reality, they were still in stasis on the Earth's surface, their consciousness now turned off. Like the rest of the planet's inhabitants, either they would never wake up from their sleep or they would be revived from stasis to find that Earth's greatest battle had been fought without them.

He checked on the nuclear arsenal that the twins had helped to launch and noted that the first bombs would start to fall very soon. An excellent bonus – the Helyions thrived in a radioactive environment. It was like pure oxygen is to a human being.

Zadra Nurmeen picked up his weapon and shot the remaining two human slaves that Pierce had procured. They'd been keeping their heads down, as they had for the past five years in captivity, trying to survive, desperate not to be noticed.

Something beeped on his wrist and he responded to a message on the communication device which he'd been using earlier. He used an alien language – nobody on board the Nexus would ever have been able to translate the content of that conversation.

On Earth there were twenty-nine Helyion ships clustered around Lake Karachay. There was still one ship missing. It would soon dock with the Nexus and be boarded by Zadra Nurmeen's Helyion army. He would not require the troopers for much longer, but he would retain a hundred or so, as a backup plan. Deactivated, of course.

It would be a short time until the cloaked ship docked with the Nexus. Just enough time to tie up a final loose end. He grabbed Harold Pierce by his hair and unceremoniously dragged him to the airlock. He didn't utter a word. Zadra Nurmeen was not like the unstable Henry Pierce – a true despot feels no need to explain himself. He threw Harold into the airlock, turned his back on him, and nodded his head to one of the troopers. He didn't even look back as the trooper closed the door, activated the external doors and blasted whatever wasn't secured in that area out into space, directly into the path of an approaching Helyion ship.

The doors were open for twenty-two seconds, but that's all it takes to jettison something – or someone – out into the oblivion of space.

CHAPTER EIGHTEEN

Remnants

The Queen knew they were on board the *ISOCell* – she felt their presence as they arrived.

The last remaining part of her not yet dominated by the machine Henry Pierce had constructed to restrain her struggled to focus on these two people. It was a woman, younger than her, and a boy. The woman was human, but there was something special about the boy.

Hundreds of messages clouded her thoughts. She was tapped directly into the minds of the entire trooper army. She was receiving commands via the console on the Nexus but now something strong was coming through. The boy … he was not entirely human. She felt a Zatheon connection with him, and it was strong.

As she fought to focus on this single train of thought among the voices in her head clamouring for attention, she struggled to work out her connection with this boy. She flashed through her fading memories which were now subjugated by the cruel treatment Henry Pierce and Zadra Nurmeen had inflicted upon her.

Then she caught it, only for an instant. She knew this boy, she recognized his Zatheon trace. A strong maternal reaction surged through her body, but it was quickly adjusted and was extinguished by the machine to which she was attached. The boy was her son. She'd seen it just for a moment, in a precious glimpse of memory, before her mind was clouded by a thousand thoughts and feelings from her trooper army.

Viewed as she was now, crucified on this machine which controlled every part of her, she looked like an abomination, a monster created in a lab. But the Queen was capable of emotion – this was an evil thing that had been done to her.

And had anybody been watching, they would have seen a single tear run down her cheek before those memories were obliterated by her distant master.

Impetuous

As the transporter door opened to Quadrant 3 and seven laser targets fixed on the two figures inside, the security team were taken aback to see what was going on.

'Kneel down and show us your hands!' the security chief had shouted, nervous about an impending trooper attack, even though Pierce's recent announcement had denied that it would now happen.

The two figures inside the elevator completely ignored

him. They were fighting. They recognized one of the figures as Doctor Pierce, the man who'd addressed them in the past hour via his ops area on the Nexus. Yet here was Nat, pounding his face with her fists, and clearly doing a good job of it.

Like all bullies, Henry Pierce was just a regular person. Once you removed his weapons, entourage and support network, he was nothing. Caught in that transporter together, it was just Nat and him. And once Nat recognized who he was, she had some catching up to do. Henry Pierce was only in his early fifties, but the force of a sixteen-year-old, six foot girl launching at him without warning had come as a shock to him. Particularly as he was already struggling to recover from a wound he'd got in the fight that had just taken place in the ops area.

Nat was angry, very angry, and she didn't stop to think how valuable this new captive might be. With only fifty minutes of life left, this was how she'd decided to spend it. While her twin was risking his life to bring resolution to the problem which was destroying them, Nat was creating a delay which might kill them both.

So hard were Nat's blows, so violent was her rage, that she'd left Henry Pierce a bloody mess on the floor of the elevator. It took three security guards to pull her off – she continued punching and screaming even once she'd been restrained.

Henry Pierce's wounds were so bad that by the time he'd arrived in the med lab, he'd sunk into unconsciousness. Had he been awake, Xiang could have shown him how he too was in peril from the nanovirus that had been released into the bodies of the hybrids, himself included, and perhaps worked towards a swifter solution.

But now, because of Nat's rage, they were no further forward and he was useless to them.

Interception

The missiles with the shortest distance to travel would fall on the Kremlin. Viktor thought of his own family. They would be among the first to perish in their apartment on the outskirts of Moscow. He had thought when this mission began that they would be safe, deep in sleep after the darkness fell and secure in their family home. Now they would be among the first to die. Maybe that would not be such a bad thing, they would feel no fear and know no pain.

But Viktor was not about to send his own family, or the people of Moscow, to the grave without a fight. He'd activated the Global Defence Matrix thanks to the data supplied by Mike and he was making headway. He looked at the missile projections on his screen. There were three minutes before the first nuclear detonation took place.

He forced his mind to focus – if he looked at all the missile trajectories shown on his screen, he'd just curl up in a ball and give up. Somehow he had to take out all of these nukes, their destructive capability was immense. If they reached the bunkers it would be 'game over' – there would be nobody left to fight.

An all-points alert came over his comms tab. Apparently they'd got Henry Pierce in the med lab now, but the crisis situation still remained. In all his concentration, Viktor had missed an earlier text alert.

'Two minutes to detonation,' came the voice on his console.

He glanced at it and gave it a quick scan, noticing the words 'Lake Karachay'. He'd return to it later. His fingers were working furiously at his screen.

When President Ronald Reagan had imagined this Global Defence Grid in 1983, it is unlikely that he ever conceived that it would be used as it was on that day. One man, alone, trying to save the world from destruction, while his friends – he felt that he could call them that now – struggled in their own battles: Xiang to save the twins, Mike to get a breakthrough which might end the sabotage, the twins to fight for their very existence and Amy who was battling to save her children.

Even if he stopped this attack, Viktor knew that the war was not yet over, the enemy would remain undefeated.

'One minute to detonation,' came the voice on his console.

A circular clock countdown appeared at the bottom of his screen. Sixty seconds – fifty-nine seconds – fifty-eight seconds ... that's how long his wife and daughter had to live. Thousands, if not millions of people would die when that first bomb fell.

Viktor typed furiously at the screen.

He was in, he could target each nuke individually now.

Forty-five seconds – forty-four seconds – forty-three seconds ...

Where is the activation system, what's the code?

'Mike, do you have any codes in your data-set for the Defence Grid?' he spoke down his comms tab, calmly but urgently.

He felt sweat all down his back, a drop trickled from his forehead onto his work station.

Thirty-four seconds – thirty-three seconds – thirty-two seconds ...

Above Moscow, four nuclear weapons separated off at right angles and fixed on their final coordinates.

'A-1-00-JKL-4897 ... that's Alpha, One, Zero, Zero ...'

Viktor cut Mike off as he completed the code. 'Got it, thanks!' and he quickly typed in the information.

No time for pleasantries now, in just seconds the detonations would begin.

As Viktor keyed in the data he recalled an event that had happened in his own military life, before he'd even had a family that he cared about. A gun held to his head, a terrible game of Russian roulette by a vindictive prison guard and a dead colleague at his side. Viktor had stayed calm then, in spite of seeing his friend's head blown away right by his side. He'd stayed calm, waited for his moment, and survived to fight another day.

Fifteen seconds – fourteen seconds – thirteen seconds ...

The code was accepted, The Global Defence Matrix was activated. On his screen, a red grid appeared around the graphic representation of the globe. Each nuclear weapon was marked and tracked by a yellow symbol on the screen.

Nine seconds – eight seconds – seven seconds – six seconds ...

Viktor slammed the activation button at his console and watched his screen. The red grid illuminated and from each nodal point on his display a green line mapped to the nukes and indicated that every weapon had been targeted in an instant.

One by one, the yellow symbols disappeared on his screen.

The Defence Grid disabled the closest to detonation first, then took out the nukes which had furthest to travel.

Two hundred nuclear weapons blown out of the skies in

an instant. There would be some injuries on the planet surface as missile debris hurtled to the ground below, but nowhere near the millions of lives that would have been lost on that day had Henry Pierce and Zadra Nurmeen succeeded in detonating those nuclear bombs.

Viktor sat back in his chair, the sweat on his shirt and forehead the only indications of the intense stress he'd just been under.

A huge cheer went up in the control room. Viktor had been so focused that he hadn't realized that everybody around him had been watching him, praying that he'd be able to make this right.

Viktor closed his eyes and thought back to the cold war of 1983 which had caused President Ronald Reagan to create the Star Wars programme. And he took a moment to thank his country's former enemy, because without that Defence Grid they would all have lost their lives that day.

Failure

At last Xiang made a breakthrough. Mike and Magnus had determined that the trooper in the med lab room was actually the twins' natural father.

She could only imagine how difficult that must have been for Mike to discover, having raised Dan and Nat as his own kids, but she knew him well enough already to know that today would not be the day for petulant obstructions. Dan and Nat would be his dead kids if they didn't all work together. They were down to their last forty-three minutes of life now.

She'd taken a moment to celebrate the news from Viktor that the nukes had been disabled, but it was far from over yet. She drew blood from the restrained trooper – Jeff, as they would have to get used to calling him now. He was in an extreme state of desolation – whatever had happened to him since his helmet was removed was causing him problems. It had been difficult for Xiang to take the blood that she needed. He was wriggling and squirming on the med lab bed, in spite of full body restraints, and his mutterings were just not making any sense.

Xiang left him to the med lab staff. She moved through into the larger room that her team had commandeered to help to save the lives of Dan and Nat. Had it been anybody else but Xiang, this might have looked sinister and threatening, but this equipment and these tables had been set up to heal, not to harm. There were two operating tables, two hover trolleys and a bed. It was the best they could do. Whoever had equipped these bunkers had not anticipated the need to carry out any complex processes like this. Xiang needed to be ready for the worst case scenario – or the best case scenario – depending on which way you looked at it.

She knew that potentially she had two groups of hybrids – Dan and Nat and the Pierces – as well as the Queen, the twins' birth mother. She now had access to the father too. She'd quickly run some tests to see if she could eliminate the nanovirus that had passed between the hybrids by accessing the uncontaminated blood from the human parent.

The fate of the Pierce brothers was less certain. She was sure that she could make it work for Dan and Nat if she could access the same hybrid DNA from a parent, but she wasn't so sure that she could do the same for the brothers.

Not now that both of them seemed to have been infected by the nanovirus.

She received a message via her comms tab – the med lab had incoming casualties. Nat was being brought in by the security team, and there was one other person with her who may be of interest to Xiang. It was one of the Pierce brothers, but he was wounded.

Two of these empty beds would now be full. She'd start to wire everybody up and begin running tests. Now she had live subjects to work on, surely success was within her grasp. She would have to work fast. Dan and Nat had only thirty-four minutes of life left.

Survivor

When the airlock doors opened there was a violent and terrifying rush of air out of the area. When the first poor soul had been flushed out into space earlier, he had counted how long it had taken – he estimated that the process took no more than twenty-five seconds.

He'd struggled to remember that part of his degree course. How long was it that a human with no breathing apparatus or protective clothing could survive in space? It was many years ago that it had come up in his studies, but he was sure it was thirty seconds. When it came to it, he knew that he'd have very little time. There was a cluster of pipework and wiring in the corner of the airlock. He would never be able to hang on in a zero gravity environment. But he was carrying a gift that had been given to him by a Zatheon friend many years ago. Then it had been a token of trust and friendship. At that moment it was to be the thing that saved his life.

The minute he'd been thrown into the airlock, he'd torn the tie from around his neck and wrapped the noose tightly around his wrist, pulling the knot firm.

As the airlock doors slid shut and he heard the activation process begin through the strengthened glass, he tied as many knots as he could around the pipework. He managed three. Would it be enough to hold onto a man of his size in a zero gravity rush? He wasn't sure, he would soon find out. Harold closed his eyes, took a deep breath and started to count. He heard the airlock doors open and as they did so his entire body was pulled with an almighty force to a horizontal level.

As the last oxygen vacated the area, the violent tugging on the tie around his wrist stopped and he began to float. He dared to open his eyes and look out into space, but his mouth remained tightly closed.

By his count it was nineteen seconds – surely the doors would close again soon?

He could feel his internal organs pounding, his tongue was beginning to burn and he was struggling to maintain consciousness. As he stared out into space, he felt himself fading fast. The outer doors slammed shut once again on his count of twenty-two seconds.

The vacuum was replaced with an injection of oxygen and the return of gravity. His body slumped gracelessly to the floor. His wrist was red raw where his body had been pulled violently towards the nothingness of space. He was bruised and sore, no longer just from the beatings of his own brother.

Harold Pierce had survived an attempt to flush him mercilessly out of the Nexus, and now he was going to start to fight back. Only he could reverse the sabotaged terraforming process, but if the Nexus were destroyed, there would be nothing that anybody could do to save the planet. It was the Nexus that controlled the programming of the shards.

He sat slumped in the corner, allowing himself time to recover. He thanked his friend Davran Saloor for her wonderful gift. A simple token, a tie made of a special Zatheon fabric. But on that day it had saved his life, and would give him a last chance of rescuing the planet they both loved.

He could see the Helyion ship approaching the Nexus for docking. They were going to connect via a larger airlock, they would not use the one he was in.

The airlock's inner doors opened swiftly without warning and he braced himself for the violence that would surely follow if they'd seen how he'd survived their attempts to end his life.

He didn't recognize the man, who was looking behind him urgently, as if there wasn't a moment to spare. 'I'm Dae-Ho,' he announced. 'Come with me!'

Legacy

Magnus stopped to draw breath. There was a lot going on, a constant stream of updates coming his way and he was beginning to feel frazzled. The trooper's helmet was still on his work area, fully illuminated, receiving communications that were no longer being listened to by its owner.

A thought struck Magnus – he wasn't sure where the idea had come from. He'd been troubled by Jeff's spinal implant, all the troopers had them. They were not unlike his own work in this area, when he'd been running cybernetics trials in the lab.

They'd come down really hard on him when he'd started to branch out into the non-military applications of his work, but it seemed uncannily similar to him, albeit a bit more brute force in its delivery. Nobody would be able to achieve this without some form of adaptive algorithm, he'd secured that concept many years ago, surely someone hadn't created their own version?

Magnus fumbled in his pocket and took out a paperclip that he kept in there to fiddle with. He bent one of the arms and used it to flick the lid off a small box that was concealed in the rear of the helmet. It was packed with micro-circuitry, but this was familiar territory for Magnus. He knew exactly what he was looking for. He found the main chip and pulled off the label that was obscuring the logo. He was right. Nobody else could have re-created his adaptive algorithm.

The logo on the chip was printed with the words 'Magnum Enterprises'. They'd used his own technical innovation to create these monsters. And now they were going to destroy him and his planet.

Simulation

Simon and Kate ran along the corridor. They could hear the heavy boots of the troopers behind them, and the flashes from their weapons struck the sides of the walls as they struggled to outpace them.

'I'm out of condition,' gasped Simon. Kate stopped to let

him catch up. 'I wish I was as fast as the first time we had to do this.'

Kate thought back to their simulation exercise all those years ago. Both of them were younger, fitter and more naive in those days. Now they had experience on their side. They would use what they'd learned in their twenties to help them survive this day. They wanted the troopers away from the ops area, out of the heart of the Nexus. They were going to be the distraction. The bait.

Nat was safely dispatched in the transporter and they'd successfully diverted the troopers in their direction. Now they just had to keep them occupied and buy time … in the hope that somebody, somewhere would do something to end all of this, before it was too late.

In the meantime, they'd create as much mayhem as they could. Kate fired at a mass of pipework overhead and a cascade of sparks shot across the corridor like a firework at a display. Simon smiled and they began to run again, Kate pacing herself so that he could keep up. They'd already prepared to die once, in the simulation exercise they'd been involved in years earlier. They'd both stared death in the face already, and they'd do it again.

As Simon's hand slammed on the pad of the simulation area, he activated the programme via his remote. The green grid lines which lined the vast hangar disappeared as the virtual renderer created in perfect detail the battle scenario they'd faced together eighteen years ago. The wire cutters were by the fence as they always had been, the camp was immersed in darkness and a rat scuttled across the yard. A laser appeared from nowhere and shot it dead, burning it to crisp in an instant.

Beyond the doors they could hear the thundering boots

of the troopers approaching, a small army preparing to eliminate the last resistance to block its path.

Kate cut the wire and Simon climbed through the fence. The battle for survival had begun.

Predator (T minus 31 minutes)

As the comms tabs faded to nothing, the transporter began to surge into life. We'd been slow, we should have known they'd follow, of course they would. We were trying to save Davran Saloor, my birth mother. They wouldn't let that go unchallenged.

This transporter was not like the others. It wasn't tied into my DNA. It was a bit do-it-yourself, to be honest. It looked like it had been lashed together on one of those TV science shows. There was a single unit in the ops area and this one on the ISOCell was almost exactly the same. You couldn't fit more than three people onto it. It wasn't for a military invasion or anything like that – I'd guess that Henry Pierce and his pal used this to get from wherever they were based to Davran's capsule in space. To do whatever they've done to her.

This appeared to be the only way on and the only way off the ISOCell, which meant we were about to be boarded by somebody – or something. I grabbed Mum's arm.

'Mum, split up! Don't wait for me – if you find Davran, get her back to Quadrant 3. Just do what you can.'

Mum nodded and as we headed off quickly in opposite directions, I thought I heard her voice calling after me.

'I love you, Dan!' are the words I thought I heard, but I couldn't be sure.

This place was much smaller than where we'd come from. It made sense, I suppose. It only needed to house one person. I hadn't even thought yet about how we could get off this thing without it exploding. If I had to, I'd stay behind if it meant Mum and Davran could get out alive. I was going to die anyway from the nanovirus, so it might as well be in this ISOCell. I was running completely blind now – I didn't know how long I had left to live. I must be down to my last minutes. I was feeling fine, but how long had I got? Twenty-five minutes maybe?

I glanced behind me and saw a figure materializing on the makeshift transporter behind me. It was Zadra Nurmeen. He was armed, but not with a gun, he was carrying a sword. He looked reptilian. I hadn't noticed that before – it was his eyes that did it. I wanted him to follow me, not Mum. She needed to find Davran and get her out of here.

'Hey, ugly!' I shouted. Zadra Nurmeen's eyes narrowed even further and he scowled at me. He gripped his terrible sword, lowered his head and set me in his sights.

Damn, I hadn't got a weapon. I'd grabbed a comms tab but had forgot to bring something to defend myself with. I hoped Mum had something to shoot him with – surely she would have been more on the ball than I'd been. That sword he was carrying had been saved for me. He might have been holding it like a normal sword, but I knew it was a much more sinister tool. This alien was a predator – and I was its prey. Well, I was going to give him a run anyway, hopefully long enough to buy Mum the time she needed.

I started to run away from Zadra Nurmeen, along the curved corridor that circled the cell. There couldn't be many places to hide here. It wasn't that big, the size of a spherical house perhaps. I was beginning to think I could outrun him when things turned against me.

Zadra hurled his sword at me, but it turned out it was more like a boomerang. It spun through the air at a frightening speed, gashing my right leg, then returning straight back to its owner. I let out a cry of pain. Jeez, that hurt like hell – I could feel the blood seeping into my trousers. My chances of outrunning Zadra Nurmeen had just reduced drastically.

CHAPTER NINETEEN

Launched

Viktor's feeling of achievement didn't last long. Magnus had got new data on the significance of Lake Karachay in this scenario. It wasn't good.

At first, they'd managed to scan the area using radar, but nothing showed up. Magnus had had an uneasy feeling about it and decided to persist. In the end, it was a heat map generated via a mapping satellite that confirmed things for him. He could see twenty-eight of them, circular clusters of heat hovering above the water. Something else seemed to be immersed under the water too, he guessed it was another ship, but its heat trace was almost non-existent. They were just waiting there, doing nothing, like a gang of hoodlums up to no good.

As Viktor looked at the surveillance images on his screen, he knew what had to be done. He hesitated as he decided whether or not to share this information with Magnus. He was used to working alone, trusting no one and resolving issues like this in isolation. That day he decided to change his policy. This small army of theirs was a force to be reckoned with – he was proud to be a part of it.

He desperately wanted to save his wife and children. They'd just come so close to death, he was not going to let that happen again. But he was going to have to take the biggest gamble of his life to save them. And he wanted to share that with his friend, Magnus, an American who had shown himself worthy of trust, loyalty even.

So Viktor and Magnus moved unobtrusively to a meeting area off the control room and made the decision that would either hasten the destruction of their planet, or help to save it. They were chasing off a group of predators, gathering like jackals, ready to devour the spoils of war.

Together they programmed in the coordinates.

Together they placed everything on a knife-edge.

Together they launched Viktor's fifty hidden nukes at a single destination: Lake Karachay, where the Helyion army had gathered, ready to take over the planet.

Free

Amy had seen Zadra Nurmeen arriving on the transporter, and she saw him head after Dan. She hesitated, thinking she ought to go and help her son, but she also knew she needed him to buy her some time. They'd come here for Davran and they were sure as heck leaving with her.

She found the Queen almost immediately, the *ISO*Cell was only small. Amy was horrified by what she saw. It was the stuff of nightmares. What she didn't know was that the experiments carried out on her own daughter had helped to create the monstrosity that was now before her, experiments which had given essential data about Zatheon biology and neurological pathways.

Davran had numerous tubes running in and out of her body. The entry points had been cut into her skin, they were messy and septic. Her head was roughly shaven and there were scars beneath the new hair growth – little attention had been given to her comfort when this happened. Electrodes were attached all over her head. She was showing high levels of distress, sweat covered her hands and face. Worse still, she was lashed to a metal frame, to keep her upright and still.

Henry Pierce and Zadra Nurmeen had committed this obscenity. They had shown no compassion at all in their treatment of Davran. Amy didn't know what she should do, but she took action anyway. First, she freed Davran from the frame that restrained her, untying the strong bindings that had been used to keep her attached to this place of crucifixion. She looked at the tubes and the wires, sizing them up, trying to figure out what purpose they were serving. Then she did the only thing that she could do.

As gently as she could, she removed the tubes from the incisions in Davran's flesh. Then she tore off the wires. Finally, she repeated a trick that she'd learned from Simon in the stasis room. She ripped out all of the cables which served the area. As she did so, the power in the *ISO*Cell died, leaving them in the darkness of space.

Amy grabbed Davran, supporting her weight as she rushed towards the transporter, their path illuminated by the dying flashes of power from the severed cables. As she touched the panel on the transporter, she saw the silhouette of Dan coming around the far corner. He'd completed a circuit of the *ISO*Cell without being caught.

She had to trust in him. She took a long final look at her son and hoped it would not be the last time she would see him alive.

Broken

Mike felt sure that the SD card must contain some important information. He'd checked out his theory when Xiang alerted him that Nat was back in the Quadrant. Nat had passed on a message through Xiang that she'd retrieved the data from Henry Pierce's computer wherever it was that they'd been experimenting on her. It seemed his best bet with time running out. He could wade through the Genesis 2 data for months and not find anything, and besides, Magnus's guys were still working on that.

Finally, after all the interruptions, Mike inserted the SD card into Amy's laptop. The low tech was a relief to him after working to get up to speed with all the new systems in the bunker, but he was having a problem. The SD card was in and the laptop was charged fully, thanks to the wireless power available throughout the bunker, but there was nothing there. The drive was displaying fine, but it appeared to be empty. Hellfire! Surely not?

Mike tapped the return button, then tried it again. Nothing there still. Nat couldn't have been wasting her time on this – there must be something on it. Perhaps it was encrypted? Then he thought back to something Dan used to say to Amy whenever she checked her emails.

'You're going to wreck that button!' he would laugh as Amy worked through her inbox, cursing the spam and unwelcome mailshots. Maybe it was the return button that was the problem.

He thumped it so hard that he feared it might damage the laptop. He was right, the data sprang into life on the screen in front of him. He looked in expectation at whatever essential data this SD card had concealed. It was just a list of four codes. They were absolutely meaningless to him.

Cornered

Simon remembered the sequence exactly. He was surprised at how much of the detail he'd retained, even though it was now almost twenty years ago. The frazzled rat right at the beginning had been genius, it helped to build up the tension and jeopardy before the entire mission went awry. This simulation area was just one big psychological puzzler and it all made perfect sense once you knew how the tramlines worked.

They would wait outside the door to the office block until the troopers had followed them in deep enough to be spotted, then they would finish it all off inside the main complex, after the rooms were mixed up – the twist that had disorientated them twenty years ago. All Kate and Simon had to do was to follow the tramlines – if you stuck to them, nothing hit you.

It was disconcerting for both of them, however. It took a real leap of faith to hold steady amid the weapon fire, the alarms sounding and the clumping boots of the approaching security teams. It might have been a simulation, but it was completely immersive and Simon now understood how they'd been herded into that final, terrible decision-making situation right at the end. By the time you got to that stage your adrenalin was pumping and you'd jump out of a window if they asked you to.

It wasn't long until the troopers entered the simulation area. There must have been at least thirty of them. The Nexus had been breached and the Queen was issuing instructions to save the nest. Simon and Kate's distraction had worked well. The Queen must have thought that her adversaries were still trapped on this ship. That would give Nat and Doctor Pierce the cover they needed to get away, and Dan too might be able to move around unobstructed, wherever he was, whatever he was planning.

Kate jumped as a laser struck the door to her side, a little too close for comfort. It was simulated fire – not from the troopers – but how would they tell the difference? Sticking to the tramlines would not save them from the troopers' shots. Maybe they should have thought that one through a little more.

'Keep to the tramlines!' shouted Simon. It was difficult to hear him over all the noise.

They just had to create some leeway, come up with a diversion, give Nat, Amy, Dan and anybody else who could make it out alive time to get back to Quadrant 3.

The troopers would focus on him and Kate. They'd left a strong enough trail of destruction, after all. They'd lure them to the centre, then, at the final moment, blow up the entire hangar. Take everybody out, themselves included, if they had to.

Kate and Simon walked through the office block door, having scrambled the rooms, as before. Both fought to concentrate on the tramlines – the distractions were enormous, everything was created to produce an affront to their senses, emotions, fears and doubts. The troopers were close behind them. Real weapon fire had now been added to the mix. It was difficult to keep calm and level-headed, even though they had a pathway through this nightmare.

There was an explosion to the left. No worries, it was a simulation, not the troopers. A laser beam hit the woodwork to Kate's side. It began to burn. Not a simulation, a real weapon. Hell, how could she tell which was which?

Something was thrown over their heads. Simon couldn't work out what it was, but he was certain it wasn't part of the simulation. There was an explosion, it pushed them both off their feet and hurled Kate violently against the wall. The simulation pixelated and vanished in front of them. Only the green grid was left, marking out the areas where the simulations would take place. In the corner, the main control console was in flames.

Of course, the Queen knew everything about the Nexus. It didn't take her long to issue new instructions to her troopers. Disable the simulation. Destroy the controls. Eliminate the intruders.

Simon looked up to see thirty weapons trained directly on him and Kate. When those things fired it would be no simulation. He steeled himself for the end. And then the troopers just stopped.

Docking

Harold Pierce looked out of the windows of the airlock towards the approaching Helyion ship. It had come to collect Zadra Nurmeen and complete their deadly mission.

The entire Nexus was in a state of confusion. There didn't appear to be anybody in command. The troopers seemed to be lost and disorientated, as if they had no orders. He needed to do what he could before they were spotted.

'Your brother, he went with Nat in the transporter,' said Dae-Ho, an urgent look in his eyes. He didn't know how to react. He'd craved freedom for many years now, but when he'd glimpsed it, he discovered he'd been a slave too long – he needed someone to tell him what to do.

Maybe this situation could be to their advantage. Henry and Harold Pierce still looked very similar. In the confusion after the smoke bomb ambush, Harold thought he might be able to gain access to the ops area. From there he could reverse the terraforming sequence ... but he'd need the hijack codes, he couldn't do it without them. He'd need his brother for those – or Zadra Nurmeen – and he didn't think that help would be coming soon.

And the Nexus, it was going to be destroyed, he didn't know how long they had, but he'd need his brother – or the twins – to help with that too. Everything used Zatheon technology, all the systems in the bunkers and the Nexus were protected by the Zatheon failsafe after Genesis 2 had begun. They'd agreed it from the start – if Earth got into any difficulties, the Zatheons would help to put it right.

Zatheon government worked on a pairing basis. Sibling pairs would have to endorse decisions and that meant no single person could do anything to harm the species. If it was needed, the Zatheons would have full access to the lower levels of the bunkers, they'd be able to initiate Unification. They were the Plan B backup, if it ever got that far.

Harold had the alert codes for the Zatheons. He hadn't had a chance to use them before his brother boarded the Nexus and began his brutal assault. He'd thought they could handle it on Earth without the help of the Zatheons. Besides, they were reluctant to get involved, they would only initiate Unification if the terraforming process had failed. In that eventuality, it would be just him on the Nexus, surrounded by the virtual forms of the world's leaders, as the Earth began to burn below. By that stage it would have been a situation of terrible gravity. The Zatheons would extract the physical forms of the Global Consortium leaders, bring them to the Nexus, and Unification would have begun. A new start for Earth and an ambitious project gone terribly wrong.

How laughable those plans now seemed. Nobody had factored in the hybrid element. His brother was thought to be long out of the picture, but he'd sabotaged the entire process.

Harold had had a last minute hunch before they'd set the final process in motion – he'd realized their exposure a little too late. It was why he'd decided to get Dan involved in this whole thing at the last moment. It was why he had lured the Tracy family with that spoof competition, taken Amy away under yet another deception, injected the neuronic device into her neck just days before the darkness fell, did the same to her old friend James, creating allies and possibilities within the bunker. Just in case he needed them. And he had needed them, as it turned out.

It made sense to have a hybrid like himself involved. Hybrids were the only ones who'd be able to access everything in the bunkers. He cursed himself again for getting it so wrong. He knew what Henry and Zadra were capable of. Yet they'd kept their deception so well hidden, he'd never suspected this sabotage.

Now he needed his brother, he was not going to use the twins for this, the risk was too great. Dae-Ho had said that Henry was back in Quadrant 3 with Nat. He had to fix that.

'Come with me,' he said to Dae-Ho, taking charge now. 'Pretend to be working with me.'

He returned to the ops area. It was mainly quiet, there were some troopers, but they seemed dazed, they weren't putting up a fight in any way. Nobody looked at him as if he were out of place. There was no sign of Zadra Nurmeen either – that wasn't good. Harold got straight to work, he had no idea how long he had left to put this right. But he knew exactly what had to be done.

'What happened to Dan?' he asked.

Dae-Ho pointed at the transporter. 'Zadra Nurmeen went too, so did the lady.'

Harold wondered who Dae-Ho meant by 'the lady'. He guessed it might be Kate, surely not Amy? He got his answer seconds afterwards, as the makeshift transporter began to light up and two figures materialized in front of them.

He saw straight away why the troopers seemed so dazed. It was Amy with Davran. Davran was alive, they'd saved her. He rushed over to them.

'What's happened?'

She eyed him warily, wanting to be certain that this was the right Doctor Pierce to be speaking to. He seemed to be fine.

'Dan's still there, Zadra is with him. I need to go back!'

'No, go with this man. Take Davran back to Quadrant 3. She can save the twins.'

'There won't be anybody to save!' shouted Amy.

'Take her!' said Harold. 'Get her to Xiang, let Dan take care of himself. We don't have the time for this. The troopers are disconnected now Davran is offline, they're no threat to us. The Helyions are about to dock, you've got to get her off the Nexus!'

Amy saw he was right. She needed to get Davran in the transporter and back to Xiang. She had to trust Dan, she had to believe that he could outwit that monster on the ISOCell. Only one of them was getting off that ship alive. It had better be Dan.

'I'll take her,' she said. 'You just make sure that if Dan is the next person to appear on this platform that you get him in that transporter and back to Quadrant 3. I'll have a medical team waiting if ... when he gets to Quadrant 3.'

Dae-Ho helped her to support Davran who was limp, confused and bloody from being torn off the machines and tubes. They made it to the transporter and Dae-Ho stood aside as the doors closed and Amy returned to Quadrant 3.

In the ops area, Harold took control once again. He put the Global Consortium leaders back online, their holographic images surrounding him as he orchestrated events on the Nexus. At first they were unsure which Pierce brother they were looking at, but relief showed in their faces as they realized that it was the right one.

He opened up a comms channel to Quadrant 3 – this was going bunker-wide – and he patched in the Helyion ship via the docking area too.

'This is Harold Pierce on board the Nexus. The Nexus is counting down to self-destruction, it will explode in eleven minutes. I will need authorization to initiate de-Unification. Do I have it?'

All the world's leaders sanctioned his request and Harold pressed some buttons on his console. There was a deep rumble throughout the Nexus. The Quadrants were disengaging.

'Magnus, I need my brother back. Only he and I together can now reverse the self-destruct process on this ship. I also need the code sequence that Henry and Zadra used to hijack the terraforming. Does anybody have any leads on that? Does Henry have any documentation on him?'

There was silence from Quadrant 3.

'Doctor Pierce, this is Magnus speaking. Is this on all channels?'

'Yes, everybody can hear you, Magnus.'

'We're sending your brother over now. He's in a bad way. We wiped out the nukes, but we've launched fifty of our own.'

Faces dropped on the holographic screens – there were visible signs of concern. World leaders were not used to having their power usurped, particularly not by civilians.

'We've targeted Lake Karachay. There's a force of some sort gathered there. They can either get off our planet or we'll take them with us!'

Harold Pierce smiled to himself. Magnus had a plan, he could hear it in his voice. He was sending a firm message without giving the game away to anybody else who might be listening. The Helyions would be monitoring this message, that's just the sort of thing he wanted them to hear.

'It's Simon, and Kate's with me too,' came a familiar voice. 'What happened to the troopers? We've got thirty of them with us here – they seem confused and disturbed, I don't think anything is controlling them now.'

'With no Queen, they must be disconnected,' Harold picked up. 'Who knows what effect it will have on them, but you need to get them off this ship fast. Take them back to one of the bunkers, Simon.'

'How long have we got?'

'About ten minutes now.'

'We're on it!' said Simon, and he left the broadcast stream.

'What about Dan?' came Mike's voice. 'Where is he?'

'Be ready at the transporter for him. Xiang, you have their mother. Prepare your med lab for her arrival.'

'He has only nine minutes left,' said Xiang. 'Doctor Pierce, you and your brother are the same. You are dying too, just like Dan and Nat. It must have been passed on through blood contact. You both have the nanovirus.'

She was trying to sound calm, but her sense of urgency was easy to detect. Harold Pierce was used to dealing with bad news, it just made his mind sharper. He was tired now, he needed to find the last reserves to end this. Only nine minutes for Xiang to get Davran hooked up to more machines and be ready to get working on Dan the minute he got back to the Quadrant.

'Keep all comms open now,' he said, knowing that as the final minutes played out they would need to remove all obstacles and delays.

He looked out of the windows of the Nexus and into space. The satellite matrix looked beautiful, he wished he'd taken more time to appreciate it. De-Unification was activated, the four Quadrants were undocking from the Nexus and their precious cargo would be spared the force of the destructive explosion when it came. The Helyion ship was connected now. He could see it straight ahead. They'd be boarding very soon, he had to rush.

He sealed off the ops area, leaving only the entrance to the transporter clear. He disabled the airlock to the Helyion ship, but knew it would only delay them for a short while – they'd blast their way through if they had to.

His brother had just arrived. Two security staff were bringing him on board, handcuffed and restrained in a wheelchair. He'd been sedated, but he was at least conscious now. Henry's DNA must have given access via the transporter – at least he'd been useful for something.

'Put him in the airlock for now,' said Harold. 'Let him see what it feels like.'

He had just four things to do and fewer than nine minutes to do it all.

Change the terraforming codes and reverse the sabotage process.

Shut down the self-destruct sequence on the Nexus.

Get Dan from one transporter to the next, the minute he materialized.

And blast his brother Henry out of the airlock.

Hunted

I was in danger of passing out, my leg hurt so much. I could hear the blood dripping on the floor. I was doing everything I could to keep moving forward.

Without warning, the lights went out. We were pitched into darkness. All I could see were the stars outside. And two green eyes which were closing in on me fast. Those eyes looked terrifying – I hadn't particularly noticed them before, but in the dark they were horrible. It gave me an advantage, though. He might have looked scary, but he couldn't track me as easily in this darkness.

I could see a flashing light up ahead – it was glowing intermittently, as if somebody had a fire lit. I walked into an open area. The flashing lights were coming from some electrical circuitry which was connected to a load of devices in this area. I recognized it immediately – it was where Davran was based when we saw her on Doctor Pierce's screen. I must have come full circle. Mum had just fired up the transporter – she'd got out of here, she must have had Davran with her.

I had to get Zadra away from this place. If he realized Davran was gone, he'd know that the last one off the *ISO*Cell would get stranded here. I'd have to lead him as deep into this ship as I could. Because I could see his eyes, I could locate him precisely in the darkness. To get him away I'd have to circle around him, and I'll have to do it with a leg that was now bleeding badly. I needed to bear this pain. I wanted to cry out, but I daren't make a sound – if he heard me, he'd throw his sword again.

I'd got my phone in my pocket from earlier, and it was still charged. I had an idea. I ducked into the side of the corridor so that Zadra wouldn't see me. He'd been slowed by the darkness, but he seemed more confident of it than I was. I held the phone to my chest so that the screen didn't show my location when it lit up. I swiftly navigated to the video Dad sent me. It was already there on the screen from where I was watching it before. I turned the volume up, pressed play and slid it across the floor, past Zadra's feet and behind him.

Dad's voice came out of the speaker and it immediately distracted Zadra. He turned, his green eyes disappeared for a moment and he threw the sword. I rushed by him, pushing him as I did so, and he stumbled. That sword was flying in the darkness somewhere. I didn't want it to hit me again.

I was past Zadra now, running the long way round back to the transporter. I needed to get to it before he did, or before he realized I was intending to make him the last person left on this *ISO*Cell. He'd be trapped.

Shoving him had worked. He was disorientated in the darkness and he missed the sword as it returned to him. I heard it drop on the floor – he cursed as he was forced to lose vital seconds retrieving it. He grabbed it and turned on me again, following me along the corridor. He was angry with me now, which didn't improve my chances of survival. I kept looking back, I knew it was pointless, but I did it anyway.

I could see his green eyes closing in on me. I must have lost so much blood, I was feeling light-headed. The eyes got closer and closer. As I tried to move faster I could feel my cut flesh rubbing and pulling – the skin was actually tearing as I ran.

I could see the transporter up ahead now. The activation lights let me pick it out in the darkness. He was getting breathless – me too, and it felt all the more threatening having him just behind me. He knew where I was heading, he sensed it, and he must have known this was now a race to be first off this prison in space.

I reached the transporter. I slammed my hand on the button – it felt like I'd touched base. The transporter fired into life, the coloured lights began to activate, this was it, the final moments. Whatever happened here would determine if I survived this thing.

I could feel myself slowing down. I'd lost a lot of blood from my leg wound. I could see it now in the light thrown off by the transporter. I'd never seen so much blood before. There was some when Nat was hit by the car, but nothing like this. While I could still think and move, there was a way out this, there was a chance I could make it. I wasn't scared any more. I accepted that this could end with my death – there was only a remote chance that I would make it out alive. The best I could do was to stop Zadra in his tracks. At least that would be one of the crazies out of the way.

He had caught up now and was standing on the transporter, ready to attack. The transporter lights surrounded us both. It couldn't be long until transportation began. It must have been seconds. I could see that Zadra was as desperate as I was not to be the last on this *ISO*Cell, and it occurred to me in that moment that there was another way. We couldn't leave at the same time, we'd both be caught in the final explosion.

I was feeling drained, the life was running out of me. I couldn't take another blow now, I'd sink to my knees if I did. Zadra raised his sword. He was going to take my head off. He was getting ready to make one massive, powerful swipe. I'd had a good run, at least. We'd saved Davran and Mum was safe, I hoped. And if not? Well, we were all dead anyway.

I saw that Zadra had begun to make his final movement. The lights were all around us now – either the sword would meet its target or we'd both be goners when the explosion went off.

One person had to stay. We weren't leaving this cell together.

I was okay with it now. I felt calm and ready to accept what was about to happen.

It would be over in an instant anyway.

Destroyed

Nobody knew where the *ISO*Cell was located in space. It could have been in any one of the Off World Federation universes. It had only been located in the first place because of a tracking device secretly injected into Davran Saloor before her punishment of ostracism was carried out. These cells were littered throughout space, abandoned and forgotten, the final resting places of whoever had been condemned in them.

Billions of kilometres away in the Veluvian galaxy, there was a sudden explosion, smaller than a pin prick in this vast mass of stars. It went completely unnoticed and it took only seconds to burn up into nothing. Just a few bits of debris floated out into space. The last person had attempted to leave the *ISO*Cell and it had completed its final task: to ensure the perpetual incarceration of the life form inside it, or to destroy them as they tried to leave.

Minutes later, in a different galaxy, there was another explosion, a much bigger one which rocked the planet far below and shook the matrix of satellites which had been formed around it. The Nexus was gone and all who were on it had perished. The Helyion ship which had been docked to it was nowhere to be seen.

EPILOGUE

Funeral

Amy always found goodbyes difficult. She choked up as the memories of Nat's funeral came back to her. Even though it had all been a carefully orchestrated charade, with no body in the coffin, it had been very real to them at the time. Here she was again. Only Harriet and David provided some relief from it all. Young children are always a blessing at times like these, they create a distraction from the misery.

They were the survivors, a small group of regular people who'd been caught up in extraordinary events and managed to save the entire planet. Amy let the rush of emotion come. The tears flowed freely now, she felt that she'd earned it. They'd been through so much together, those who'd survived, and the world was having to piece itself back together again.

She knew she would never be able to tell the full tale, just like the time she'd been caught up in the army exercise which had nearly ended her life the first time. The truth about what had begun in the Secret Bunker would need to remain hidden, the world would have to believe that this carnage had been caused by a devastating solar flare, a natural phenomenon, rather than inhabitants from other planets.

She squeezed Mike's hand hard as the final words were spoken by the minister and the coffin was lowered into the ground. Simon nodded at her, acknowledging all she'd done to fight this, to protect everybody involved. They'd succeeded – the fact that they'd come together for the funeral service was confirmation of that. None of them felt as if they'd won a victory though, with so much loss of life.

Kate stood by Simon, and it was good to see Magnus, Xiang and Viktor there. They were all bound by these terrible events and they would be for the rest of their lives. Many people had attended from the bunkers, it was as if they had to be there, as if it was one of the only ways they could cope with what had happened.

The coffin was lowered into the ground.

Amy waited a moment, clutched Mike tightly, and they walked away across the graveyard.

For somebody who had just helped to save humanity, she felt a bleak sense of emptiness.

Survivors

Mum and Dad went to James's funeral. Nat and I were mad that we couldn't be there, but if they detached us from Xiang's device it would cause us big health problems. Apparently. They probably just said that to scare us, to make sure we stayed hooked up to it.

We'd have liked to have attended the service. We didn't know James that well, but we all understood that we owed him our lives. If he hadn't disabled that mobile phone mast it was hard to think how we might ever have won our battle.

My leg was still painful. It had been stitched and bandaged, but I hated the way I could feel where the two bits of flesh were trying to heal. I was reminded every time I made a sudden movement. I was still experiencing bursts of emotion, where I wanted to cry and scream, but I was trying to keep them to myself. Nat could feel it, our connection was so strong now, but she finally seemed to have learned some patience. She was waiting for me to tell it when I was ready.

I wasn't even sure myself what had happened in those last seconds. I could remember the transporter lights flashing and seeing that sword heading at speed towards my neck. It was hazy now, but I recalled a surge of rage before I moved to push Zadra Nurmeen off the transporter. I guessed he thought he'd got me, so he wasn't expecting it. I must have managed to push him off just as transportation took place. Or maybe he tried to follow me and was blown up as he tried to leave the ISOCell. Either way, Nurmeen was the last off the ship. He was the one who got caught in the explosion.

I made it back to the Nexus by the skin of my teeth. I didn't recall much after that, just glimpses, like Dae-Ho rushing over to me on the transporter. That was my last thought actually, because I realized that if he was there, and not a trooper, they must have re-taken the Nexus while I'd been away. And Mum must have made it out alive too. Another flashback of Doctor Pierce. He didn't have a tie on. I was so out of it I couldn't work out which of the twins it was. Then a medical room, and Xiang's face. After that, nothing. Not until I woke up stiff, sore and confused in a med lab. I wasn't sure which Quadrant it was, but I was alive. And very pleased about it too. Nat was with me, and through the glass, in a separate room, the guy they called Jeff. Nat told me she had some big news to reveal about him, but she was sworn to secrecy until my strength was up, and I couldn't sense it, even though I tried. I'd lost a lot of blood and I was lucky to be alive, according to Nat. Didn't I know it?

We had a lot of catching up to do. I was looking forward to it. It felt like renewal, a chance to put everything behind us and move on. Most of us had made it out alive. I couldn't pretend to be upset about Zadra Nurmeen or Henry Pierce. They got what they deserved, although Dad told me some things about the Pierces which make me wonder about Henry – it sounded like he had a pretty rough deal. Nat and I needed to be grateful we hadn't met the same fate. It could have been one of us on that drugs trial. Even so, things hadn't been easy for Nat. We'd all had some rough treatment from the Global Consortium.

I couldn't wait to get out of this place now – I was fed up with living underground. But they couldn't move us anywhere else. We needed Zatheon technology for the healing process to complete, and that couldn't be revealed to the outside world. It was just another little secret that the public would never get to know.

I didn't reckon I would ever hear myself say that I needed to get outside into the fresh air, but it was all I could think of now, cooped up in this hi-tech, artificial environment.

Oh, there was another great thing about finally leaving this place too. I couldn't wait to get my hands on a decent wi-fi signal again.

. . .

The Final Seconds

In the end, it took just seven minutes to determine the final destiny of the Earth. Seven minutes in which any other sequence of events would have forever changed the future for the billions of lives on the planet below.

At seven minutes, Mike opened up his comms tab and spoke to Harold Pierce. Something he'd said earlier had been troubling him. It was about the terraforming codes – could that possibly be anything to do with what was on the SD card? He'd found four codes, they seemed useless to him, but might they be what he was looking for?

At six minutes he sent the files over to Harold and at five minutes Harold confirmed they were the codes to give him access to the sabotaged terraforming process. The sabotage was reversed in an instant as the codes gave him back control of the shards on the planet surface.

At seven minutes Magnus and Viktor had watched as the twenty-nine Helyion ships had powered up and begun to leave the planet. All fifty nuclear weapons were less than three minutes away from blowing them all out of the atmosphere. Viktor held steady right up to ninety seconds before detonation. He wanted to be sure they were leaving. Then he activated the Global Defence Matrix and blew every single missile out of the skies. The sentinels in space found each target, fixed on it and rendered each one immediately useless. He hadn't needed to use the nukes after all, but the gamble had paid off.

By three minutes, Simon and Kate had managed to send any remaining troopers back through the transporter to

Quadrant 3, where medical teams were ready to care for them. They were confused, delirious even, but harmless now that the poisonous stream of orders had ceased transmitting. The troopers' helmets gave free access to the transporter. The evacuation process was fast and efficient.

At seven minutes Xiang had attached the final tube to Davran, who she'd had to sedate due to the extreme disorientation that she was experiencing since being detached from the machines that controlled her. A series of tubes and wires connected Davran and Nat, but there was an empty bed for Dan. It needed Dan for the process to be complete.

At four minutes, the transporter in the ops area on board the Nexus sprang into life and the swirl of lights obscured the single form that had just materialized on the platform. Dae-Ho picked up a weapon discarded by one of the troopers and pointed it at the figure. It was Dan, bleeding badly and looking bruised and exhausted. Dae-Ho shot the controls of the transporter, to be sure that nobody followed after him, then threw down the weapon.

Simon and Kate had stayed behind to wait for Dan. Between them they loaded him into the main transporter and sent him back to Quadrant 3. By one minute he was wired up in the med lab and the healing blood from his unconscious birth mother helped to save the son and daughter that she had not seen for over fifteen years.

As Simon had gone to activate the transporter, he'd shouted to Harold, 'What about you two?'

The brothers were the only two humans on board the Nexus. The troopers were either heading back to Earth in one of the four Quadrants or they'd been evacuated by Simon and Kate.

'We'll follow you!' Harold replied. Simon nodded and took the last party back to Quadrant 3 in the transporter.

As the transporter door closed, Harold heard the thud of Helyion boots stomping along the corridor. It was too late, he didn't have time to reverse the self-destruction sequence. If they caught him now, they could change everything and regain the initiative. That wasn't going to happen.

The nukes were disabled, the terraforming was back on track, Dan had escaped the *ISO*Cell, the four Quadrants were heading back to Earth, and he'd just heard from Viktor that the Helyions were leaving the planet's surface.

Two minutes left. They were dead anyway unless he got back to Quadrant 3, along with his brother. He'd let his brother go once before, given him the benefit of the doubt. He was too dangerous to be locked up in a prison or incarcerated somewhere humane. The Helyions would only get to him again. Henry was unable to stop himself.

Spurred on by the approaching Helyions, Harold Pierce picked up his E-Pad and walked towards the airlock. He typed in a series of three codes that only he knew, and then smashed the E-Pad against the wall.

He walked up to his brother and kissed him on the top of his head. His eyes moistened as he walked up to the airlock door and keyed in the activation code. The airlock doors opened and the two Pierce brothers were flushed out into space, dying almost instantly. As they drew their last breaths, the Helyion boarding team reached the ops area, where all was quiet. The holographic images of two hundred of the world's leaders watched as the alien life forms looked around, bewildered by the scene that greeted them. Then the self-destruct sequence reached zero seconds and the Nexus and docked Helyion ship were blown into tiny pieces, joining the two Pierce brothers in their cold dark grave in space.

As the massive explosion ripped apart the two space

craft and several of the surrounding satellites, an armada of Zatheon warships appeared just outside the bright lights of the matrix. They'd received the three codes sent by Harold Pierce only moments before. They'd finally come to help their friends from Earth. They were going to escort the twenty-nine Helyion ships back to their own planet and far away from this solar system. And they were going to make very sure that they never came back.

Reborn

The Earth was reborn, though fewer than three thousand people would ever know it. Officially, it was solar flares which had incapacitated the world for the past seventeen days. Hurriedly, the world's leaders, relieved to have survived these events, agreed on a containment and misinformation plan. They'd just escaped the tragic consequences of their own scheming, yet here they were again, covering up, fabricating untruths, changing reality to appease the population of the planet.

Fewer than one million people perished in all. It was a terrible loss, but nowhere near as bad as it could have been. The world had been minutes away from total extinction – now it had been reborn, billions of human lives were saved. Nobody felt a sense of victory, though. This battle had been won at a terrible cost.

And if it wasn't for a group of civilians who'd been thrown together in the heat of crisis and created such a remarkable fighting force, this would have become a dead planet. Home for an aggressive Helyion race intent on mining its rich mineral deposits and allowing the human inhabitants to perish in a sabotaged environment, their dying screams unheard.

The four Quadrants had returned to their hiding places below the bunkers, complete with their cargo of embryos, weaponry and troopers. The ethics of that programme would be argued about in private for many years to come, but it remained intact, a subterranean ark, hidden out of sight should mankind ever need it again.

The terraforming process was successfully completed, thanks to the fast thinking of Harold Pierce. He perished on the Nexus, alongside his twin brother, but his final gift to the planet was the one that he'd intended to bestow all along, ever since he'd become involved in the Global Consortium – that of sustaining life on Earth.

The rebirth of the Earth would continue, undetected by humans, and using nanotechnology borrowed from the Zatheons. This technology was developed by an expert mineralogist called Davran Saloor, a much respected citizen of Zatheon who'd once been ostracized for crimes against the Off World Federation, but who was now fully pardoned in recognition of the terrible suffering she'd endured in the battle for Earth.

Afterwards

I couldn't believe that we'd returned to this place a year on, but I guessed it was only fitting really – where else could we go to remember the people we'd lost and the events we were caught up in?

I was walking with Nat across the car park and towards the cottage. We all travelled here by traditional means –

there were no transporters involved in this gathering, just cars, taxis and aeroplanes. And there was also the occasional helicopter, laid on by Magnus, of course.

My leg still twinged occasionally, usually when I swung out of the car, but most of the time I wasn't really aware of it. I noticed that the mast James blew up across the fields was back now. After a year to recover, there wasn't much evidence of what had gone on across this landscape – just a few grassy mounds and rocks deposited where they weren't previously.

The bunker staff greeted us as we arrived. Troywood was closed to tourists – it was only open for people who were here for Genesis 2 today. We'd all shared a unique experience. I was changing my mind about this gathering now I was here. It was a good thing to do.

We all moved through the bunker entrance and gathered outside the bunker's blast doors. Everything was as it was when we first came here on that family day trip, completely oblivious as to what was about to happen.

So much had changed in the past year. It had been an amazing time for me and Nat. We finally met our birth parents – Davran and Jeff – and now we felt like we were part of a big, happy, extended family. It made no difference to either of us that we had two mums and two dads, we treated them all the same, although we were still getting to know our natural parents.

It took a long time for the Zatheons to put Davran right. She was a wreck after Mum rescued her from the ISOCell, but things were now coming good for her. Jeff too had had a tough time of it. They were both pulling through. It seemed to really help when they were around everybody else in the family. They were struggling to know what was real and what was implanted by the neuronic devices, but being rooted firmly in reality only helped that process.

What a change there had been in a year.

Dad now worked for Magnus at the recently expanded Magnum Enterprises. He was a chief coder there, managing multiple teams. He still did most of it via the kitchen table, mind you, and always had time for an online cat video, but working remotely he was doing some great things these days. He'd updated and refreshed his tech skills. His new role had given him a new lease of life.

Magnus looked like a different person too. He rediscovered his passion for helping humanity through tech innovation and was adapting his sabotaged exoskeletons to help people with mobility problems and paralysis. He was determined that something good would come from what we'd been through.

He'd brought in Xiang too. He thought they'd be able to make the leap to bioskeletons fairly soon, as well as developing a way to bridge spinal damage using nanotechnology. Xiang seemed to have found her natural place as well. She was looking really happy that her work was being used for only good projects now, her conscience was at peace.

In fact, Magnum Enterprises was expanding in some very interesting ways. Viktor now headed the newly created agri section, developing his own research to adapt it for areas where crops struggled to survive. Magnus reckoned that within three years they'd be able to feed starving populations in regions hit by drought and floods, adapting the processes that Viktor developed to grow crops in seawater and in darkness.

It was all really cool tech, the stuff of sci-fi, but that was my world now. It went with the territory – I had an alien mum after all. My two mums got on really well, and we called them by their first names so we didn't get confused. Even though they're both still 'Mum' to me and Nat.

Amy and Davran had become political activists – it was great to see Amy using some of that kick-ass attitude again. Without a weapon in her hand, of course. They gave the Global Consortium a hard time after Genesis 2, and with the blessing of the Off World Federation, they'd won approval for increased ties between Earth and Zatheon.

There was even agreement that everybody on Earth would know about off-world life forms within the next ten years. It would be a staged process, which my mums would oversee. That was an amazing prospect – by the time I was 27 there could be Zatheons on Earth and out in the open. That would bring some big changes for me and Nat. We'd have to decide whether or not to keep our alien heritage secret, but that decision was a long way off. We needed to see how the world reacted to news of alien life forms first.

Amy and Davran also forced the Helyions into submission via the Off World Federation courts. They were completely neutered now – my mums proposed a new process of 'recalibration', where planets using technology for aggressive purposes had their expansion limits curtailed and strictly monitored. Put simply, their entire planet had been clamped. Everybody agreed – what the Helyions had tried to do could never be allowed to happen again. It was humane, but decisive, just the sort of thing I'd expect from Mum – Amy. They'd helped to re-write the Covenant.

Simon and Kate were here too. They now led the work of the Global Consortium, jointly replacing Harold Pierce as its head. The world's leaders owed everybody such a debt of gratitude, it all made perfect sense. Besides, the key task of the Global Consortium had been accomplished and they could move on to new projects now. Simon and Kate were determined that those projects would be about creation, growth and sustainable development. They'd vowed to change the ethos of the Consortium and to be more open about their work.

Even Dae-Ho was there, with his family. Nat rushed straight up to him and wrapped her arms around him. Those two had shared some horrible history that I was never a part of. I'd heard Nat's story now. It was difficult listening, but I was sure she was putting it behind her. She was just pleased to be back with the family. A wonderful extended family, which included lots of new friends.

We were missing Harold Pierce and James. They should have been with us, but they'd sacrificed their lives for this, they'd helped us save the world. They weren't forgotten. James's family was there, it was good to meet them at last. Amy visited regularly and kept in touch. She still felt guilty about James, I'm not sure why.

The bunker had been restored to its original state, the incredible transmogrification enabled by Zatheon technology now reversed and concealed once again. Hopefully, the bunkers would never be needed again and they'd remain tourist attractions.

Magnus unveiled a plaque in memory of James and Harold and there was a spontaneous round of applause. The plaque couldn't say what they did – the wording said, 'They cared deeply about this planet' but we all knew, we remembered what they'd done.

I looked around this gathering of family and friends, standing on the edge, needing a few moments alone to sort this all out in my head. I'd spent twenty-four hours trapped by those doors in complete darkness, petrified that I was about to lose my mum and the rest of my family. I couldn't exit until I'd done what was expected of me. Well, we did it, together, and it was worth it, I think.

I wandered off towards the café – they were serving food and drinks so it was on my list of essential stop-offs. There was a newspaper on one of the tables and I leafed through it casually, thinking about Magnus's offer to me and Nat. Neither of us had gone back to school, it seemed a bit superfluous after what we'd been through. It's a bit difficult to think about anything nine to five after you've lived through the final battle for Earth.

Magnus wanted us all to move over to the States and work for him out there. He said Amy and Davran could base their political work in his offices so we could all be together. It was just what we all needed, a big change to help us all to settle again. He wanted Nat and me to work in the company, eventually to run it with him, he hoped. I knew we'd say yes to him. I could feel Nat jump with excitement as soon as he mentioned it to us on the web chat.

So this was probably the last time we'd gather in Troywood. I wasn't sure I'd want to mark the anniversary every year. It was right to do it on that day, but we all needed to move on. Yes, I had decided. I was going to join Magnus. I'd liked him from the minute I met him and I wanted to get involved in his projects, and work alongside the team on the exoskeleton project. With that decided, I grabbed a cup of coffee and skimmed the paper, not yet ready to do the socializing thing.

It was amazing how fast the world returned to normal. The headlines were dominated by reports of the aftermath for about three months, then bit by bit the celebrity stories returned and before you knew it, it was like nothing had ever happened. Humans have an amazing capacity to fill the voids that are left behind by tragedy – I guess that's why we've done so well as a species. We just get on with it, however bad things get.

So it was no surprise to see the latest celebrity gossip on the front page. I had to move a few pages in until I got to the story that really caught my attention. It was only a few column inches, a fraction of the size of the celebrity story, as if it didn't really matter. It was a simple headline, and I nearly missed it. I thought it was all over, but I realized at that moment that it never really ended.

The headline was there for all to see, a warning if they only chose to heed it, and it suddenly felt like we'd learned nothing from all of this:

New Subterranean Gas Source Discovered

Power Supplies Secured 'For Centuries' Scientists Reveal.

AUTHOR NOTES

Author Notes

You made it!

Congratulations, you now know the answers to all the secrets, who's a goodie, who's a baddie and what was going on with Doctor Pierce. That's all the loose ends tied up - but if you've got any unanswered questions, just get signed up at https://thesecretbunker.net/mail and shoot me a reply to the welcome email, I'll be delighted to answer any queries that you have..

I really enjoyed writing that book, I was so excited at the end I couldn't type the words fast enough. It would look great in a film, wouldn't it? It was all imagined cinematically, I've obviously spent too much time at the cinema watching Star Trek and Star Wars films. So, who were you gunning for in the book - and did you get any nasty surprises?

And what about those aliens? If you pushed me, I guess I'd have to say that the Helyions are probably a mix of the Klingons and the Ferengi - more in attitude than appearance. The Zatheons are calmer and more cerebral, like the Vulcans (but with more emotion) and Star Trek's Dax, who's a Trill. I liked the idea of symbiosis, but I handled it in a completely different way with Dan and Nat and the Zatheons.

So, the big question is, will there be any more? I've already told you that Magnus appears elsewhere in my sci-fi, as does Harriet (but blink and you'll miss her!). I love time travel stories and I do have a plot outlined which picks up right where we leave Dan at the end of Regeneration, on his own, sitting in the cafeteria.

Remember the scene in Terminator where Arnie says 'Come with me if you want to live'? And in Back to the Future where Doc says 'Marty, you've got to come back with me ...'? Well, it's based on that premise, where a key character comes back from the future to take Dan away from the Bunker's cafeteria into a brand new adventure that will push him to his limits.

There are clues in Phase 6 - check out what happens to Magnus in that book. Oh, I've also got a space opera sketched out too - featuring a half-completed spaceship and a dying captain who get caught out when the planet goes dark in Book 1.

So many ideas, so little time to get them written!

Are you now desperate to check out Scotland's Secret Bunker? If you do get a chance to go, don't miss out on it, it's one of the best visitor attractions I've ever been to. Let's face it, it must be good if it inspired me to write three books about it.

By the way, I should mention that the whole concept of The Grid Trilogy was inspired by the simulations area in The Secret Bunker. It's the same universe, same tech but with much more sinister uses.

Did you shed any tears in the book? I hope so, but only in a nice way.

I always remember the episode in Star Trek: The Next Generation when Tasha Yar died. It was before the end of Season 1 in the episode titled 'Skin of Evil'. At the time, nobody ever killed off main characters in TV series, it was unprecedented when it first aired. I like to kill off main characters in my stories, as a reader, I like to feel that anything could happen. I was genuinely shocked when Tasha Yar died and I like to try and write in a few of those scenes in every book, whether I'm writing a thriller or sci-fi.

So that's it, the end of The Secret Bunker Trilogy. If you're desperate for more, read Phase 6 next, then move on to The Grid Trilogy. And, now I've given you some big hints, keep an look out for when I open story threads and don't close them, they're all put there for a reason.

Thanks so much for reading the books, if you want to check out the last of my CLASSIFIED features - complete with big spoilers - just head for https://thesecretbunker.net/3-secrets

Thanks for reading the trilogy and I hope you'll stop by another of my stories sometime soon.

All the best, Paul Teague

ALSO BY PAUL TEAGUE

Sci-Fi Starter Book - Phase 6

The Grid Trilogy

Book 1 - Fall of Justice

Book 2 - Quest for Vengeance

Book 3 - Catharsis

With Jon Evans

Book 1 - Incursion

Book 2 - Armada

Book 3 - Devastation

ABOUT THE AUTHOR

Hi, I'm Paul Teague, the author of the The Secret Bunker Trilogy and The Grid Trilogy as well as several other stand-alone psychological thrillers such as Burden of Guilt, Dead of Night and One Fatal Error.

I'm a former broadcaster and journalist with the BBC, but I have also worked as a primary school teacher, a disc jockey, a shopkeeper, a waiter and a sales rep.

I've loved sci-fi all of my life, starting with the Danny Dunn books and progressing to the huge franchises such as Terminator, Star Trek, Babylon 5, The Hunger Games and The Maze Runner series.

Be first to hear about new books and special offers:
https://paulteague.co.uk/
paul@paulteague.com

Copyright © 2019 by Paul Teague

All rights reserved.

No part of this book may be reproduced in any form or by any electronic or mechanical means, including information storage and retrieval systems, without written permission from the author, except for the use of brief quotations in a book review.

Printed in Great Britain
by Amazon